Bleeding In

CW00377095

All material Copyright © 3B publishing 2023
All rights reserved by Sarah Jane Huntington

Bleeding into New Worlds

'The path away from carnal pleasure, away from bodily desire is a most dangerous walk. There is great risk to spirit, sanity and flesh, yet at the pinnacle of heightened exquisite pain, a veil parts, a door opens. Wonders await, untold delights that few can ever comprehend.'

The Peeler of Layers- The Book of Hidden Fragments

NOW

*A*nna Chambers grips her ritual knife firmly, admiring, for a moment, how the shiny blade catches the pretty amber flames of the flickering candlelight around her. The sharp edge holds promises, whispers of illicit secrets, and salvation. Her body, decorated with intricate, painted-on symbols, shivers with rich anticipation.

The purpose of the special blade is to slice her skin wide open.

She doesn't need to prepare for the onslaught of her own horrific pain, she welcomes the brutal agony and waits to embrace it.

Forbidden paths lead to redemption, absolution lies ahead.

There is purity in pain, she thinks. *There is purity and release within exceptional levels of pain.*

Power too.

Words of lessons taught to her and remembered. Warped instructions and commands etched into the layers of her brain.

She lifts her flowing skirt and finds a tender piece of flesh on her thigh. Her skin is not smooth and unblemished, but instead, already scarred and heavily mutilated by her painful past.

She doesn't mind the sight. Each scar captured a past moment in life, a punishment, or a lesson she once thought was essential.

She understands now that there was never a need to harm herself or issue such severe penalties onto her own body. She was never the one deserving of torture, of such fierce judgment.

Hindsight is a wonderful thing, although it brings its own fresh waves of misery, its own private symphony of sorrow. Alternative views of the past are forever slanted, and crooked for any future onlooker.

The suffering she now endures by design is different for her, beautiful in its own pure way, purposeful, and sacred.

Besides, the most wicked scars she possesses are carved deep into her emotions, her feelings, and bitter history, but she can escape every callous wound embedded in the fabric of her physical body.

Her real self, her true essence, her soul, she believes, is trapped, contained within a human shell, a meatsuit prison, a house she wants to leave and discard.

Astral travel. Astral projection. Out-of-body experiences. Flights of energy beyond infinite imagination.

There are secret worlds to explore, albeit temporarily. Layers and dimensions hidden away from human knowledge and greedy, calculating eyes. Dreamscapes of wonder, mighty lands of wild depth, and vivid mystery. Multiverses. All possibilities must exist. Higher realms are alive, and she can reach them.

Those are the teachings of Kingdom House.

She will bleed her way into new worlds.

Ritual is the shining beacon, the flare that signals intent, and escape. Secret words whispered with passion and meaning invoke hidden doorways. A veil parts. Pain is the key with which the door to elsewhere unlocks control is to be divine.

The mind is the most powerful weapon a human being can own, there is originality, and unlimited potential contained within soft tissue, neurons, and cells. Consciousness is capable of wild adventures beyond set barriers. The ultimate transcendence, a journey only gods and not fools dare to make.

I can do this.

5

One deep breath of sweet expectation is all she allows herself. She presses the sharp blade against her skin, and slices deeply.

Blood immediately rises and cascades down her leg in a tide of red.

She doesn't see, she is lost in the feeling. Agony, a singularity of. A brightness few stop to comprehend.

Endure.

Horrific pain can cause madness with its extreme and violent nature, but there is more too. Hidden inside the force of agony is the clarity of perception that must be held and used.

White-hot sensations ripple across her nerve endings and make her jerk wildly.

Purity in pain.

There it is, that quick flash of bright fierceness, that spark she needs. The essential moment of unbearable heightened and blurred perception. Something inside her loosens, and the curious chain that binds spirit with flesh begins to uncurl.

She concentrates desperately, needing the release. If she could just catch the edge of awareness, the outer limit of discernment, she will be free. She will explore, she will lose her bodily anchor. Great insights await.

Delights draw near, pleasures beyond all meaning, closer, closer.

She knows the door to elsewhere is present and its nearness feels like a tease, right within grasp and yet not.

Frequency, vibration, change.

As agony rips through her body, so bitter it verges on blinding rapture, her spirit begins to lift, trained to be forced out of her body. Subconscious fights consciousness.

Panic begins as a single flicker and takes hold, insecurity, and fresh doubts of flame. Her rational mind fills with fear and prevents the escape of her spirit.

The pain is not enough to temper her worries and she comes crashing back down. Eyes open, aware, still chained to her physical form, trapped.

I'm still here.

Disappointment swarms like a whirlwind.

Another failure. Now what will she do? Her shame feels crippling, an apocalypse of melancholia.

Broken birds with clipped wings will never fly, will never leave their gilded cage of decaying bones and filthy rot.

A single tear slides down her face, just one, yet alone it carries the weight of a thousand more.

I'm a failure.

"You have such little faith," a deep voice in the darkened corner tells her. The owner of the smooth velvet voice is Alex James

7

Palmer. Master, teacher, and everything in between. A beautiful man with dark contradictions for a soul.

"You don't truly believe," he adds.

His words are untrue and verging on spiteful. Anna *does* believe with every atom of her being. It is the familiarity that keeps her grounded. The limits of agony are set far too low. Her entire history, the foundation of herself was created by hurt and cruelty.

Pain for her is ordinary, an established fact of life. Agony is her companion, if not her friend. She knows true brutality all too well. Her own memories and uncertainty keep her trapped and stuck in the house that is her body, not doubt or lack of belief.

"I need more," she answers. The shake of her voice reveals her true desperation.

"Ritual knives are never enough. Cuts and slices, it's no use. I've self-harmed my entire life. Until I overcame it."

She adds the last sentence as a show of defiance and strength. She doesn't want Alex to misjudge her as weak. For all his illicit knowledge, he jumps to conclusions with alarming regularity.

"The teachings, Anna. Purity. There are rules to true freedom, to frequency change."

"Yes, I know, but…"

"You lack focus."

"No."

"Infinite realms exist within the same spaces as us. Our vision is restricted, we're blinded until we shift states."

"Again, I know."

The conversation is recycled, words spoken between master and student many times.

Anna feels a bubble of hot fury rise. The lessons Alex teaches now feel patronizing, repeated explanations told to her as if she is a small child. True skill doesn't always follow understanding.

I can do this; I know I can.

She is aware that tonight is one of her last chances, if not *the* last. She has no place in the big house if she has no proven ability.

While others visit exceptional hidden worlds, she remains left behind.

She clenches her fist, digs her nails into her palm, and lets her new thigh wound continue to bleed. Let her blood empty out of her, what does she care? Let it drain away until only a corpse is left, perhaps then she will truly be free.

"One more try left Anna, one more and then…"

Nothing else needs to be said. Yes, she knows. She will have to leave and return to the wicked reality she hates.

The mundane, the ordinary, the nothing that was her life before the group found her wandering like the stray and feral cat she was.

Alex stands, disappointed no doubt, and exits the darkened room. The candle flames flicker in protest and now she sits alone, with only anger for company.

Rage. Another old friend. Hello darkness.

I have to do this; I can't go back to my life that was.

How could normality ever compare to almost becoming extraordinary? Nothing in human experience could ever compete. She would forever be the woman who almost touched divinity and at the last moment, failed to reach and fell instead.

Fire swarms the emptiness inside until her body quakes. She knows she has the ability; her soul has travelled before.

I'm not a failure, I'm not.

No, she will not be removed from the place she considers home. She will achieve glory even if it kills her and there is no death. The end is nothing more than a clever illusion.

I can do this.

Alex promised her, he swore she was gifted enough to astral travel with the group, to leave her body and fly. His quick words and luring nature, his order in a society of random chaos, his plans and dark beauty, his father's rituals, and dusty old book, a grimoire from a time long ago.

"Pain is the release," he once told her. "In order to free a soul. The pinnacle of heightened exquisite pain."

Were his words a lie? Pretty gift-wrapped promises and nothing more?

No, she does believe. She's seen another realm before, glimpsed otherness.

She lays down on the soft mattress and closes her eyes. Her new cut stings like wildfire but it isn't enough to free her, the depth isn't severe enough.

Cutting, slicing, she is an old hand at such mutilation. Meditation, ritual, focus, fasting, and training her body, can't have all been for nothing.

I need more, something unique.

There is too much at stake to fail.

Anna thinks back to that first day, months before, to the magic that was in the air, she could feel it vibrating like a heartbeat around her. The memory is precious, it was the day she was seen, the moment her life changed.

Fate and the universe collided and arranged for her to meet the family she so desperately wanted and needed.

It all began with Bethany. Sweet Bethany and her glorious sunshine ways.

THREE MONTHS EARLIER

Anna, as always, is lost.

She knows where she is, on the main high street in a city she's lived in for years, wandering paths she's walked a hundred times or more. She has a small and basic bedsit of her own, a repetitive, dull job she hates, and still, she cannot find her place in the world and never truly has.

Born screaming and unwanted, rejected from her very first breath.

She is tainted, marked by emotional struggles those around her can sense and know to avoid, lest her misery spread and infect them too.

Today is a Friday, the day everyone around her adores simply because it means two days away from work.

Life seems inherently unfair. Die inside for five days a week, live for two, repeat endlessly. Obey the system. Earn enough to keep a roof over her head and food in her belly in a capitalist world. Struggle.

She knows something more must exist besides basic survival.

There is an atmosphere in the air, spread by passers-by in layers of desire and excitement. The tendrils of happiness fail to reach out and touch her and instead, draw away.

She walks alone, miserable, ignored, unseen, unnoticed.

Two options face her. Either she can stay in her bedsit all evening, with tired television shows for company, or she can visit nightclubs in search of mayhem, drugs, drink, and empty sex. Anything she can get her hands on to numb her, or anything she can use to feel something other than overwhelming despair.

She could dance wildly and lose herself in thudding music, surrounded by the bodies of sweating strangers. But it's all the same. It's what she does every weekend.

Nothing she ever sees excites her, no person has ever made her feel truly alive. No drug alters perception enough, no substance she ever tried can remove her from herself.

The thought of finding a high bridge to jump off occurs to her. Perhaps she could be free and fly, if only for a moment of time. Or she could journey to the ocean with heavy rocks in her pockets and let the waves take her someplace far away.

Sometimes she wonders if she is already dead. A grey person in a world of colors.

A ghost unable to see what it is they truly are.

An awkward shape trapped in an existence of perfect circles, a fork in a world of smooth spoons.

As she walks, deep in thought, an eclectic-looking bookstore catches her eye.

Perhaps she can find a book she might become lost inside? Dusty pages could work to transport her elsewhere. Or she could find a self-help book that might truly make her brand new.

She could be the equivalent of a beautifully feathered phoenix bird, born brand new from the words and teachings of others without the fire and ash.

She's tried many self-help guides before with no success. Nothing works. Lies on paper are more permanent than the ones that slide so easily from human tongues, and more damaging when such lies are revealed.

She steps inside the gloomy bookstore and listens to the tinkling bell above her head. It sounds light and pleasant, a nice way to greet a potential customer.

The scent of incense immediately assaults her, strong and tangy but not at all bitter.

Aside from a bored-looking older woman reading at the counter, Anna appears to be alone.

"Hello," the woman greets without looking up.

Anna only nods in reply and begins to browse. She can take her time, she has plenty to waste, a lifetime.

A horror section? No, she has seen enough vileness in her life already.

A row of new-age books captures her attention. Crystal healing in five easy steps? Absolutely not.

Witchcraft for beginnings? No. Cursed objects? No. Accounts from those who died and saw heaven?

Heaven.

Anna feels a sharp pang of jealousy.

She slides the book off the shelf and examines the pretty cover of lilac clouds and a bright sun.

The blurb on the back tells her the book is about people who died briefly and returned with stories of the wonderful afterlife they were able to briefly visit. Flowers grow, the blurb says, pretty flowers grow and bloom in heaven. Roses and Lilies, beautiful things, wild meadows, and happy reunions with deceased relatives take place.

"It's rubbish," a gentle voice behind her announces. "That particular book should be placed in the *fiction* section."

Startled, she turns and finds herself staring at a woman roughly her own age, smaller than her and with wild blonde hair that frames her face like a dandelion weed.

The woman is pretty, with a cute button nose and a sly grin.

"Is it?" Anna answers.

"Yep. Do you have an interest?"

"In what?"

"Out-of-body experiences?"

"Oh, yes, I suppose so. I had one, I think."

Anna cringes at her own words. She didn't mean to speak so freely. But no one ever pays her any attention. Eyes are on her and her alone, the sensation makes her feel as if she might be alive after all.

The woman narrows her eyes, curious, and looks for all the world like a wild predator about to pounce. She tilts her head with interest.

"Did you have an accident?" she asks, "And they brought you back?"

"No. Not really."

"Then what happened?"

"I'd rather not say," Anna tells her.

The woman caught her off guard and now she will close the doors of herself for protection.

Besides, what use would it be to tell a stranger about her suicide attempt? For the majority of her life, she's been craving death and yearns for the end to arrive.

Once, she believed only nothingness awaited her, oblivion, but as she died, she also did not.

"Okay, no pressure," says the woman brightly. "I'm Bethany."

Anna notices the woman carries the scent of sunshine with her. Her yellow dress evokes feelings of hot beaches and ocean waves. She looks sweet and charming, a bright light in a dark and dreary world.

"I'm Anna."

"Hello Anna, do you believe reality is not what *they* tell us it is?"

"I'm sorry, *they*?"

Bethany laughs and sounds not unlike the tinkling bell over the door. Anna finds herself to be both mesmerized and confused.

"Yes they, the patriarchal, capitalist, vile and oppressive system in charge. The ones who blind us."

"Oh."

"Come with me, there's someone I want you to meet," the young woman invites.

This is too strange.

Anna woke up with the feeling today would be no ordinary day. An extra sense inside her told her so, an ability she keeps largely hidden.

"Come on, I don't bite," Bethany grins.

"No. Sorry, I don't know you."

"Oh, that's a shame. Okay, it was nice to meet you. See you in another life. Bye."

What the?

The woman turns away and vanishes behind a tall bookcase. Anna, open-mouthed and unsure, simply watches her go.

Stop her.

A light just went out in the world and now existence feels darker than it ever did before.

Intrigue and curiosity compel her to move.

There is something extraordinary about Bethany. She has grace and carries a kind of freedom and energy she can only ever dream of possessing as her own.

She isn't one of the many, the nine-to-five workers shuttling around like cattle every day. She is different. A flash of bright colour. A spark on the dull surface of life.

Follow her, her mind tells her.

Anna replaces the book and races after Bethany. It seems urgent that she finds her. The loss of her exit is too great, it was a mistake to let her go.

Bethany has not wandered far, in fact, she is standing outside the bookstore smiling, waiting, and expecting her.

She holds out her hand, beckoning with promises.

"Let me buy you a drink."

"I don't…"

"Come on. You're safe."

Don't go with her. Yes, go!

One angel, one devil, each balanced precariously on her shoulders, whispering advice frantically.

Hadn't she wanted to experience something other than monotony? Hadn't she wanted to feel alive? *Take a chance.*

"Okay," Anna replies. "Just one drink."

What harm could it do?

And so, it begins.

The pub Bethany leads her to has newspaper plastered across the inner windows. It looks abandoned and half derelict. In need of a serious paint job or wrecking ball.

For a moment, Anna wonders about her own safety.

Somewhere within the depths of her own despair, she understands she doesn't care.

She feels more alive than she has in many years.

Something unusual is happening, something to take her away from her tedious existence. A break in the wicked dullness that is her life.

Bethany pushes the door firmly and it opens with an appropriate horror movie-style creak. Inside, dust flies up and spirals like tiny galaxies caught in the light of the sun.

'*Kingdom House meeting,*' is written in a black marker pen on white paper and stuck on the outer door. It flaps in the wind and falls.

"Wait," Anna immediately says. "This isn't some religious gathering, is it?"

"No. Not at all."

"You promise?"

"I promise. We peel back the layers."

"You do what?"

Peel back layers?

Her words make little sense. An unsolvable riddle.

Bethany grabs her hand and pulls her inside, into what she anticipates will be gloom and dust.

The interior is brighter and cleaner than she expected, the opposite of the outside. The bar appears shiny and new, polished severely. New and full bottles of alcohol line the back wall while a circle of seven clean-looking chairs and stools sit in the center of the small room.

Three people who look quite similar occupy the seats. One older woman with long grey hair tied in a neat plait, one smart-looking man in a suit and blue tie, and one younger man, slouching and with a lazy smile across his sculpted face.

Anna's eyes meet his, and a jolt of electricity passes through her. He is certainly beautiful to look at but there is something more.

He has power, a real presence, a magnet of a man.

He is otherworldly, just like Bethany. Neither belongs in the room. Still, he has that look that life has been a breeze for him, a self-entitled arrogance she finds unsettling. This is a man that causes suffering, and never receives it.

No, don't judge. Give them a chance.

The knowledge that her life is about to change swarms her. The quick sensation makes her sway.

"What do you want to drink?" Bethany asks and walks behind the bar casually. "I'm guessing…vodka and orange?"

"Oh, no. Whiskey please."

"The hard stuff! Okay, a double?"

Despite her nerves, Anna laughs and shrugs.

"Sure, why not."

She must work here? Does one of them own this place?

"Take a seat, I'm Alex," the slouching beautiful man speaks. The texture of his voice is smooth, languid, and has surprising authority and wisdom. "Bethany is my sister. This is Matt, and this is Isabelle, friends of ours."

He gestures to the people sitting beside him, both of whom nod in welcome.

"I'm Anna. So, what is all this about?"

21

She decides right then that if religion is mentioned, she will leave. No one locked the door, she checked.

She believes nothing of any God who allows such vivid chaos in the world, such disparity. Holy books and beliefs in an almighty, in her opinion, are responsible for the wicked state of society. For wars and acts of terror, for corruption and the subjugation of a woman, the acts of vileness against the innocent. Sanctioned murder in the name of some shapeless entity in the sky, one that demands blood and death. Fairy tales.

Patriarchal systems are built upon perversion, lies, and falsehoods. A control mechanism for society and little more. Bethany, she feels, was right about that at least.

Anna also has no desire to be part of a cult, even one with such a beautiful and charismatic leader. Although she does hunger for illicit knowledge, an insatiable appetite that won't be satisfied, she yearns for facts and not falsehoods.

Alex stares at her as if she is a thing to be studied. He raises an eyebrow and smiles in that lazy way she first noticed.

"You want to know about us?" He asks. "Curiosity killed the cat, or so they say."

"I'm not a cat. Yes, I want to know. Please."

22

The earth is moving under her feet and yet the ground stays firm and still. The walls ripple, and yet nothing changes.

A sense inside her tells her to run. She ignores her vital instinct and refuses to be intimidated or afraid.

"Freedom," Alex tells her. "We're here because we rebel against order and structure. We're explorers. Do you long to be unchained? Do you long to see reality for what it truly is?"

He sounds like a cliche television advertisement selling a useless product, or a parody, but his words carry weight somehow.

"Yes," she says, in all honesty. "Yes, I do, but…"

"Then sit."

Anna does as she is told without any thought. Bethany hands her a glass of whiskey, the good kind too, and with a single chunk of ice floating aimlessly on top.

"Anna had an out-of-body experience," Bethany announces and sits by her side. "She's one of us. I knew we'd find our fifth today."

Anna gasps and jolts in her seat. What happened to her was private. No, she hadn't requested her experience remain a secret, but still, it's not something she feels able to talk about. She has no real idea of why she said it in the first place. The words rolled out before she could stop them.

People already find her weird and awkward. She wants no more rejection.

"Tell us about it," Alex smiles

"You're among friends."

"It's not...I...I don't..."

"We won't judge," Matt speaks for the first time, a low rumble of a voice. "Did you see something beautiful? A higher realm? What was it like?"

Anna's cheeks flame with heat. Sweat erupts and quickly trickles down her spine, making her flinch.

They won't understand.

She has an audience before her, eager faces all gazing at her. All s*eeing* her, all waiting. Pressure. Boiling points. The spotlight is on her and her alone.

"Anna," Alex prompts. "Tell us what you saw, please."

There is kindness in his eyes, old wisdom he is far too young to possess. Knowledge of the impossible. He is so very compelling, alluring, and captivating.

Bethany reaches across and holds her hand. Her skin is soft and smooth, unlike her own. She has a cool touch, soothing.

"Tell us," she echoes.

Anna decides she has nothing of value to lose.

24

"Not higher," she speaks. "I think…I think I went… lower."

She whispers the very last word in shame.

Yet no one laughs or makes a joke at her expense. No one begins to say that it all happened inside her mind only. None jump in to say she's crazy or unbalanced, delusional, or full of lies.

Only the sound of silence follows until Alex sits up straighter and leans forward, his eyes wild and bright. Greedy, eager eyes.

"Tell us. Tell us everything."

Hypnotized, compelled, comfortable inside her own skin, and for once, half alive, Anna does.

$\mathcal{I}$t isn't hard for her to conjure the fierce imagery she needs, the scenes she witnessed have never left her memory. Even in her nightmares, she sees the world she briefly became part of.

"There was a black and white world, like an old, ruined film, you know, with hissing static and jagged, hazy clips that seemed...I don't know, spliced together."

Anna waits for her audience to nod or show understanding, they only stare, transfixed, seemingly caught in the powerful net of her words. Her story would be an unbelievable tale to most, but seemingly not to the group gazing at her.

"It was almost two-dimensional in that place, flat, I mean. Creatures flew in the sky, huge birds that looked as if they were from the Jurassic era. But they looked like cardboard cut-outs, fakes. I could hear screaming, shouts of pain, and sorrow. True misery, everything was… amplified. The fear, I could taste it. I was dead for less than a minute, but hours passed in that place. I walked and there was fire, I think…and it was white hot. The ground was made of glass shards and rusty nails. I could feel, and I could hurt. There were so many people, or shadows I guess, just wandering alone, they looked like spilled ink, but I…"

"Were you afraid?" Bethany interrupts, peering at her intently.

"Yes, of course. I was terrified. I felt…abandoned I suppose. Life had no meaning there. I felt discarded but I knew I didn't truly belong."

Besides her doubts and revulsion over speaking such truths, it feels good to talk so freely, so honestly without judgement or the heckling laughter she half expected.

"And then you were brought back?" Alex reaches out and pats her hand. His touch feels like the hissing static she spoke of.

"Yes. I was saved. I tried to tell a doctor days later, but he said it was a delusion. A common trick of the mind or a vivid dream. The brain, he said, plays cruel tricks on the dying."

"But you know it was real?"

Anna struggles. It's impossibly hard to transcribe her feelings into words that carry the true meaning she needs. How can she explain something so personal, a thing that occurred to only her?

She chooses not to mention the curious entity she witnessed inside that world. The dark, charred figure that was as tall as her, lined with sharp fins and surrounded by puffs of fresh smoke. It needed her, wanted her for some darkly sinister purpose, she sensed its intentions, its violence, and disregard for essence. As soon as Anna became aware she was being stared at and assessed, followed, she was revived and yanked away.

The place she visited was the very fabric of misery and when she returned, alive once more, something inside her was loose.

"It was more vivid than now, more real than actual reality somehow. I dream of that place, and I wonder, is right now a dream, or is it *that* world, I mean…Which one is truly real? I have nightmares about the white fire, it swallowed people, I mean…shadows that used to be people. I saw it. Life is but a dream, people say that don't they? Life is but a dream."

Anna, with a shaking hand, lifts her glass to her lips and swallows a huge gulp. The burn works to calm her nerves and soothe her tension-ridden limbs. Images and memories flood her mind of the pure white flames devouring rippling shadows until only nothingness remained.

"How did you do it?" Bethany asks.

"Sorry?"

"Attempt suicide. You said you didn't have an accident, so, I'm just guessing."

"Oh, I…I cut my wrists. I was…it was a bad time, I wasn't thinking straight, I was ill… I didn't…That's not…What I mean to say is that…"

Alex holds up a single hand to silence her rambling. She feels her cheeks flame with scorching heat.

"Do you want to die?"

"No," she says. "Not anymore."

Anna is not sure if her words are a lie, the answer she gives isn't as black and white as it should be. She wants to live, yes, but not be trapped within the current life she has. It's hopeless and lonely, so very lonely and there is no real point.

Sleep, consume, work, obey, and die.

Alone.

The only freedom she owns is her imagination and it's tainted, memories she despises creep in and ruin any fantasies she can conjure.

She is in a world full of conflict, corruption, and war.

Freethinkers, those against oppression, and people blessed with a beautiful mind are a dying breed. Everyone seems to be addicted to cell phones, all believe what they are told so blindly. It is all she sees. A contagion of narcissism. Hearts and likes are all that matter to most. A worship of self and neon billboard fake gods.

Nobody stops to ask themselves the big questions that matter. The what, why, how, and who. Anna understands no one and in return, believes no one understands her.

Her difference acts as a repellent. The perfect looks needed to navigate society more easily did not think to grace her. She views herself as ugly or plain, far below average. She always longed to be beautiful, another dream far out of reach. Like many, she is unseen and overlooked.

Alex leans back in his chair and raises an eyebrow, regards her. There is no expression of distaste on his face, no look of horror she finds she expects to see.

"The pineal gland," he says. "Have you heard of it?"

The sudden change of topic makes her brain glitch.

"I think so. I don't know. Maybe, yes, in a book or something."

"It's a tiny gland in the brain, the seat of spirit. It produces a natural substance called dimethyltryptamine upon death. DMT for short. I believe, as my father did, that DMT works to free the soul, that's its role. Either permanently, when the body dies, or temporarily when taken. Plants found in nature can cause similar out-of-body travels. Ayahuasca, is the plant shamans use for example. My father found that these hallucinogenic substances, combined with the brightest agony possible, can transcend barriers and send our energy, our consciousness, further into hidden realms than ever before. Experts call such visions mere hallucinations; we know these experiences are real. You travelled to a place you expected. Do you understand? You expected to be sent somewhere dark and horrid, and there you were. You must believe you deserve such a place."

The words of Alex cut too close to the bone; his explanation feels correct on a level she can't explain. Like attracts like. All she's ever known are bad situations and suffering, of course, she expects both to continue. Happiness has never thought to touch her. She doesn't know what such a thing feels like.

Wait, brightest agony?

"Agony?" She echoes.

She picks the word that strikes her the hardest, the word she recognizes the most.

"Yes. Pain. There is a thin line between pleasure and pain, a brief moment when the two become confused. Senses are heightened, and brain activity becomes alive. We can transcend at that moment, and we do. At the pinnacle of heightened exquisite pain, a veil falls, a curtain parts, a door opens."

"A veil? A door to where?"

"Different layers. Higher dimensions separated from us. Our destinations are pre-set by our rituals."

"And you've done this?" Anna asks, incredulously.

At her words, the group smiles. A thousand emotions swapped within a single glance. A secret club she is excluded from, an outsider.

"Several times," Matt interrupts. "And I'm the newest of the group. Alex taught me everything I know."

Matt looks more like the manager of a local bank, not a man that sits so straight, talking of astral projection as if it is all second nature and entirely rational.

"I'm sorry," she says. "I'm not sure I understand any of this. It's all just too bizarre."

Dangerous too, or worse, delusional.

Alex crosses his long legs. He doesn't seem annoyed by her questions and lack of knowledge. His eyes are bright and wild, his smile sly, villainous. He is enjoying his role as a leader, the centre of attention.

"We use rituals," he tells her. "Ancient teachings. Meditation, focus. Pain. We cross the boundaries of space and time. We become as Gods are, we become divine. We have old secrets to share, forgotten wisdom. There are doors to other places, call them what you want, parallel universes or simulated constructs. We know how to open those doors. Temporary death."

"How did you learn this?"

"From a grimoire, The Hidden Fragments, an old book my father discovered."

"Discovered where?"

"In an old antique store in Cairo. Although the book itself is from ancient Iraq."

"Oh."

Anna drinks the rest of her whiskey in one go. Her senses feel dulled and shaken.

It's all nonsense, it has to be. Magic books, self-mutilation, hallucinogens, and rituals, how can it all be true?

It just isn't possible. It has to be wild stories, lies, and twisted tales to tell in the dark with campfire flames burning to set the perfect scene.

She should get up and walk away. Leave the small pub and return to her bedsit room alone.

They are a cult.

And yet the meaningful words of Alex do *feel* real. Somewhere in the core of herself, she knows he speaks dangerous truths.

The different worlds he speaks of, she's seen one, her admission was true.

It happened three years ago, and the experience has been woven into the fabric of herself. She was twenty-four years old when it occurred and was destroyed by life and everything in existence.

In one single week, she lost everything. Blow after blow rained down until she drowned in waves of endless chaos, a bottomless pit there was no way out of, a sinkhole of despair.

Her partner, her fiancé of two years left her to live with her best friend.

We're in love, they said. *We're sorry.*

As if a few syllables carefully strung together could repair the damage done. The trust she'd worked so hard at was shattered, and her future exploded. She had no idea and failed to see the truth happening under her nose.

Yet the cold betrayal was only one of many, a last straw.

Before she lost her home and the only two people who claimed to care for her, she was full of trauma, overloaded by grief. A life spent without the essential anchor of a family, a life spent in abusive foster homes, never wanted, never valued, and not once shown any kindness or love.

Life is pain, existence is suffering. Anna came to believe fate had singled her out. A cosmic joke playing out at her own expense, or karma from past lives hitting with force.

On her last night in the home, she once shared with her fiancé, before she was due to leave, unable to pay the rent by the wage of her job alone, she opened her wrists and calmly waited for life to be over.

Except, there was no end, no oblivion, no exit. Not even a light at the end of a tunnel. Her consciousness did not die, it only moved.

Her ex discovered her, a simple twist of fate, chance, or destiny. He returned to collect the last of his belongings and found her dying.

And twice as a child, she rose from her body and floated close to the ceiling. She remembers the bare light fixture, the peeling paint, and network of dusty cobwebs. Of course, she was told it was all nothing but a dream.

What if this really is true?

"Where do you live and work, Anna?" Alex asks.

"I'm sorry?"

"Where do you live and work?"

"Oh, in a bedsit. I work in a factory, it's mindless but… You know, it pays the bills."

"Do you enjoy either?"

"No, of course not, I mean, who does? Look at the world, it's horrible."

"Do you have any family or someone who cares for you?"

His question makes her uncomfortable. She should lie and say yes, the truth makes her far too vulnerable. She is alone in the world and not one person would notice if she disappeared. Someone would replace her in her job and her bedsit would have a new tenant within a week. But lies are used too easily, too quickly, and often spoken with regret following close behind.

"No," she eventually answers. "No, I don't."

"Do you sense there is something more than all this, this materialistic ego-driven world?" He sweeps his hand in a wide arc as if the walls of the small pub are responsible.

"Yes, yes, I do, but…"

She is standing on a precipice. The edge of a cliff. She is about to fall or fly.

Down or up. Which way to go?

"Come and stay with us," Bethany says. "We have a big house, our father's house. We're quite wealthy. We own this pub too. Come and stay, just for a while. We need a fifth person. It could be you. Matt is a new guest too and look, he's fine, he's thriving now."

Anna, conditioned to be cynical, flinches at the invitation, cringes at the luring siren song.

Matt nods his head and smiles widely.

"I'm pleased I took a chance and joined," he admits. "Believe me, you won't regret it. It's all true. Every word, I swear it."

Anna certainly wants no more regret or the curse of *what if* infecting her.

What do they want from me? A fifth?

"I don't understand," she says, simply because she does not. "In exchange for what? What do you mean?"

"Loyalty," Alex answers. "We expect nothing but loyalty and hard work from you. We'll teach you real freedom and the rest, we can explain in time."

"It's too good to be true."

Everyone has a dark agenda, good things don't happen to me, do they?

"Try us, Anna. This isn't a cult. This isn't about sex either; I find such actions dull. We seek finer pleasures elsewhere. In higher realms only."

Higher realms, what would they be like?

Now what?

"You can leave at any point, you won't be a prisoner," he adds. "And you don't need to worry about money. Anything you need will be provided."

Anna is constantly worried about money, no matter how hard she tries, ends won't meet. She is paid weekly and after a few days, there is never enough left for her to buy food and eat properly. The majority of her wage is taken by her landlord, and she lives in the cheapest place possible. She can't recall the last time she had spare money.

It would be wonderful to eat good food and not panic every day.

Path one. Back to her bedsit or out to some cheap nightclub for even cheaper thrills. Come Monday and she'll be back at work, stuck in a repetitive job artificial intelligence could do better and likely soon will. Day after day stuck inside her own head, a place she hates with a fierce passion.

Or path two. A mysterious option to take, a new opportunity without obligation.

Do I have anything to lose?

Anna lost everything she once thought she possessed, including herself.

Deep down inside, she believes she is already damned, she can feel it.

Which future faces her?

One of relentless suffering, profound misery, and chaos? Is she looking at a singularity of chance, a moment of destiny, or has fate finally given her an opportunity?

She knows there is never a true ending. Death is not finality. The visions she saw when she died were not false, not delusions.

Could she spend eternity in that wretched place? No.

Higher realms. He said higher. And at any point, I could leave.

Two paths. Two futures. Which one should she take? Her inner senses scream at her to run and never look back.

I can't judge the future on the past, can I?

What if she walked away, lost her chance, and never saw them again?

"Okay," She whispers. "Okay, I will."

And so, her fate is sealed.

NOW

Anna lies on the mattress, sobbing gently, aware that her blood is soaking through the soft padding.

She wipes her face, rolls over, and finds bandages in the drawer by her side. She wraps the wound tightly. It isn't such a bad cut, although it probably needs stitches like her other slices.

For three months she has lived inside the walls of Kingdom House.

An almost mansion now owned by Alex and Bethany. There are six bedrooms in total, two living rooms, one dining room used purely for rituals, three bathrooms, and a vast garden full of fresh vegetables and fruit Isabelle tends to and grows.

Unless the group is fasting, she eats two or three times a day and eats well.

The home is clean and cared for. Surfaces are wiped, and floors are hoovered. Clothes are washed and put away. Each bedroom has a bed, a cupboard, and a simple wardrobe.

Nothing is asked of her, aside from cleaning duties which are shared with everyone.

Time is taken up by the classes, and the occult lessons Alex teaches. Sigils and symbols, rituals and tough, often harsh lessons in self-control. The training of mind and body.

The strange language Alex has them all learn is the most difficult thing to grasp, it feels alien on her tongue, dusty and guttural in nature.

Bethany teaches yoga and meditation, and Anna understands it all in theory but can grasp the practical side of none of it. Her mind will never be silent enough, will never be quiet enough to still.

Her four companions are singular in their goals.

Despite her struggles, she does not want to leave, ever.

Frustration rises, she sees what comes after life, why can she not see it all again?

Payment to travel should not cost her permanent death.

Bethany claims they have all explored many faraway realms with the aid of rituals, hallucinogens, and pain. She herself reported amethyst crystal mountains of spectacular size and colour, purple skies, and vividly clear oceans. The substance can unchain consciousness, pain is the fuel to drive a soul higher and higher. Frequency and vibration, doors open. Ritual and special words set their destinations. Endless worlds and perhaps even alternate timelines.

There are rules cast in stone.

Steps must be taken. Structure and order.

Alex insists, commands that the first astral travel must be achieved without the aid of DMT or hallucinogens in order to prove ability, natural skill, and full control of the spirit.

Minds must be strong, he says, the energy of the soul must be focused and genuinely gifted.

Layers exist. Forbidden levels.

She must peel them back alone and find her own door.

Anna wants to see wild new worlds. In temporary death, she can find true life, meaning, and possible answers. She wants to witness unlimited beauty and craves such a view.

Around her, the candles still flicker. She stares blankly at the flame and wonders.

41

Fire, it is such a simple yet complex energy. Able to give life and steal it away. A simple wind could destroy the flame, or let it run free and multiply. Water is its natural enemy. Nature in perfect balance and harmony.

Is she the equivalent of the flame, unable to burn brightly? Restricted and wrapped in wax.

No, I could try again right now.

There is always heavy pressure under the watchful gaze of Alex, pressure to perform. Yes, she will be breaking the rules but if she achieves leaving her body, then she will surely be forgiven.

And what of the ritual words, the violent syllables, and incoherent sentences Alex had them all memorise and chant? The symbols currently painted on her body too. It's all done for protection, he claims, for power and access.

She doesn't know if she believes in magic words, or modern tongues speaking ancient forgotten languages. Is that her issue, a lack of belief like Alex claimed?

"No," she whispers. "I do believe, I do."

It must be true, the power in the words works for the group. Matt is a new member and he managed just fine.

One more try. One more.

She must rid herself of rationality and fear. She has natural gifts, two special skills to aid her. The burn of infinite rage she keeps hidden inside and an extra sense that once used to help keep her safe or give her advanced warnings.

I've left my body before; I can do this.

Anna brings to mind Bethany's teachings. She pictures her body anchored to the earth by a complex web of tangled tree roots, enriched with glowing vitality. She empties her mind of all renegade thoughts and instead, focuses on doors opening.

Entrances and exits, tunnels made of stardust and vast clouds of energy. Frequency, vibration. Her soul can fly. She is pure energy.

Astral travels are a natural state. Higher levels are accessible.

Energy can alter shape and form. Pain is the key to extraordinary transcendence. Agony is sheer will, the very peak of sacrifice and suffering means to shift states. She knows this. Her body has been severely trained, her consciousness knows to lift at the very peak of heightened distress.

Soul escape.

She cracks open one eye and finds the hilt of her shiny ritual blade, already stained by blood. A curious sense of wonder grips her, finality.

Her body hurts but she can leave it. Her soul belongs to the infinite, and her essence can be set free.

Worlds await her, new opportunities.

Emotions can be left behind along with her different kinds of pain, the turmoil of failure, disappointment, and fear.

It can all be gone.

I can do this, I can.

No eyes are casting judgement. No shame is present. No pressure that is not her own. She holds the blade against her chest and without hesitation, slices deeply.

The agony is quick and sharp. The peak of pain almost feels like a sexual climax. Her spine arches, while her mind fills with white-hot fire and flames.

She gasps loudly, breathless, lost in pure unfiltered hurt. Still, it is not enough.

The wound she has made is rapidly bleeding, open, raw, and far too familiar.

The intense and exquisite peak she needs is lacking.

Her body sweats furiously as an idea strikes. Flames.

She wants to burn. Fire can be her friend.

Burning flesh would be a new idea. Enough to separate the anchor that holds her down.

44

She takes her small lighter in her hand, the one used to spark candles, and lights the flame.

One, two, three.

Determination is a powerful force; she is utterly cornered.

Flame meets raw open flesh. The pain is more bright and vibrant than she ever imagined was possible. Nerves on fire.

Purity.

One flash of absolute purity.

Clarity.

In pain she finds redemption.

Her hand shakes, and a battle commences between mind and body. Every nerve, every cell is telling her to move her hand, to let go of the flame that burns. Her flesh smells rancid, and blisters form with haste.

She will not give in. She understands she will succeed before it happens, her extra sense tells her so.

Her entire being begins to spasm. Tears flow freely. Black spots burst across her vision and the room starts to spin wildly.

Longer, longer, hold on! I must.

The pain reaches a higher climax. An unbearable threshold has been crossed. A barrier cascades down.

Madness is close, biting and snapping at her heels.

She focuses, she is in control, no one else, just her.

She is all and nothing, beginning and end, alpha and omega.

Don't let go, hold the flame.

Blinding agony.

Anna feels a lift, a jolt, a snap, a loosening inside. Her vision turns grey, and colour flees and hides.

Awareness increases and stops, time pauses briefly. She stands on the edge of a metaphorical cliff, about to plummet. Her insides crackle and hiss. A fierce jarring sensation hits her, a rip or tear yet she can think clearly.

Anna is still in the room, the one that is her own for the time being.

She moves slightly, a reflex and it is then that she fully understands. Her body, it's light and strangely different.

There is no pain.

She tries to stand quickly. Her movements are smooth and graceful, not the clumsy ways she is ordinarily prone to. A drift and not a stumble.

She turns and, on the bed, breathing softly, eyes closed, it is her.

Euphoria erupts, excitement, and a sense of glorious freedom.

I did it! I really did it!

She examines herself with eyes she does not physically possess. How broken she looks, how thin and scarred. Empty.

How meaningless. A temporary flesh prison.

She looks down at her new self, she is translucent, glorious, flowing white energy with threads of vibrant blue streaks flashing inside.

I'm still me!

She still has her memories, her knowledge, her full awareness, and feels full of wonder.

The shimmering room begins to feel hostile, a menacing cage somehow. She glides to the window and peers outside. It all looks the same as it did with physical eyes, only grey, with subtle shades of black and white.

Where am I?

Another layer.

A thin silvery cord is attached to her, springing forth from the place her stomach should be. The other end is attached to her physical form. An umbilical cord for a new level.

It looks for all the world like the tether of an astronaut locked onto a spacecraft.

She knows what it is, what it means.

She will not stray too far; her astral cord will prevent her as long as her body is breathing and alive.

Can I explore outside?

No sooner does the idea occur than she moves. Out through the window, solid matter is no obstacle, not for her.

She cannot feel any wind, heat, or cold. Only pressure, like diving deep underwater.

Caught in wonder, she turns and spins in the air, moving in an arch, dancing in mid-air.

I want to go up.

Up she goes, higher and higher until her cord refuses to stretch any further. She stops with a jerk and bounces back on herself, spinning wildly.

True freedom.

It is the greatest pleasure she has ever known, the purest. Excitement quickly rises.

She can see an outline beneath her, the barely-there glowing shape of her legs and feet. She wiggles her toes and witnesses only a sparkle, a shimmer.

The ground is far below, with the intricate winding path to the house present, along with a few familiar cars parked in a line.

This world is the same as our own?

How can that be and where is she?

She gazes around. The same countryside surrounds her, but the tall trees are dead and decaying.

A shadow world, a shade, where am I?

48

Fields that are usually ripe with wheat are piles of rot. Vast and thick cobwebs cover spiky and spiteful bushes.

The sky above her is a light shade of grey. There are no clouds, no way to tell if it is night or day. There is no sun and no moon, no pretty stars to attempt to reach and touch with a single fingertip.

It is a place that seems to be little more than an echo and beautiful in its own deceased way.

She floats in midair and laughs with disbelief. Astral travelling will be her addiction. The more she leaves her body, the longer her cord will stretch, according to her lessons and one particular ritual makes it vanish altogether.

She is more alive, more real than trapped inside a human body.

Movement catches her eye. She pauses, shaken and in awe. A creature, a wild beast of magnitude, swims lazily in the sky, its movements are similar to a whale in the ocean. The lizard-like being pays her no attention and drifts past, its gaze fixed on something far away and out of sight. Its large and scaled tail almost touches her.

What is this place?

Worlds full of wonder. She wants to explore more and wills herself to drop down lower, slowly, and gently until her energy touches the ground. Her new environment makes little sense, it feels dead but yet life exists. She is light, without mass and still, her feet are real enough to feel.

Different dimensions, accessible layers.

She walks slowly, creeping with intent and curiosity. Hanging on the nearest tree is a warped and melted clock. Its hands are low and tired, its numbers are almost gone.

What does it mean?

Two burning amber eyes watch her from the twisted branches. She jolts and gasps.

A beautiful white owl assesses her without real interest. It spreads its feathery wings and takes off, disappearing out of sight.

What is an owl doing here?

The atmosphere ripples and shimmers, as if an earthquake or soundwave is striking the air.

What a bizarre world.

In the distance, at the end of the long twisting path of the house, she sees a tall figure standing completely still.

Who is that or what is that?

Anna wants to know; she wants to see. Surely nothing can hurt her in the form she is in? At least, that's what Alex repeatedly told her.

She moves quickly, excited, running at speed without the exhaustion that would ordinarily strike. The figure is as tall as her, hooded, and draped in dense black cloth.

"Hello?" She says. The word sounds flat, as if she has spoken underwater. The figure moves, one single movement, one step towards her.

Run. Run away now.

The black cloth falls away as she stares, frozen into place, desperate to see what lies beneath. The unveiling causes a snap inside her mind, and terror rises. The being is made of evil incarnate and charred flesh. Zig zag lines of orange lightning writhe and spark inside it.

Tendrils of smoke curl away and make elegant spirals in the air. Fins line its entire form, lethal and razor sharp. Its eyes are bright blue and full of rage and loathing, hate and bitterness so vile she can feel the energy of disgust.

It is the entity she saw previously when she briefly died, she is certain. She knows it somehow.

Anna feels her mind untether. Images bombard her, pictures of a pure white soul being ripped apart and devoured, entire planets turned into rotten wastelands. Human beings screaming in eternal anguish. Flowing lava and molten metal oceans in turmoil. Fire, unstoppable flames.

Its nature is to destroy, she knows this much, and can sense such a thing. One piece of charred, blackened flesh falls off it and hits the ground, smoking wildly, as if made from acid.

'*Revenge.*'

It speaks inside her mind only and the word is hissed. Tendrils, ripples of emotion spread out, waves of dark light that attempt to touch her. Instantly, she is repulsed and jerks back.

Get away, her mind screams.

The figure steps towards her.

Anna spins and runs, her translucent feet barely touch the ground, and her thoughts are on fire with wild panic. If it touches her, existence is over, her sanity will break beyond repair, she feels sure. Up she goes, flying high, needing any escape she can find.

From behind her, a sound erupts.

The deep bellow of a trumpet, or ship's horn in the midst of thick fog.

Desolation approaches.

The noise feels like a declaration of war, a warning of an imminent attack.

Anna hates this place, this world of menace and dread.

She was taught that beauty lived in other worlds, not evil and hatred.

Leave this realm.

She holds her tether, her cord with her translucent hands, and uses it like a reverse climbing rope. Down and down, she tumbles, back in through the wall, into her familiar room.

52

There she is, her body, still alive and still breathing.

Quickly, quickly.

She is a warrior woman now, able to make sacrifices in order to transcend boundaries. She has meaning. She belongs with the group and deserves to live in Kingdom House if she can stay alive.

The loud sound bellows once more, closer, nearer.

Anna concentrates. A reverse is needed. She remembers her lessons to relax and push away all panic.

She hovers above her sleeping form and tries to merge. She fails. Once, twice, and a third time, she cannot join and simply slides through herself.

Dread sets in. She does not want to be here when whatever it was she encountered finds her.

I can do this. I know how. Be calm.

Slowly, slowly. Like putting on a familiar glove or worn old shoe.

She only has to relax. Life is but a dream, she must remember.

She understands she has succeeded the moment she feels heavy. Pain immediately strikes and then she is certain.

I'm back.

Soul and body are one again. The separation is over, she has returned, and she is safe. Her limbs feel clumsy and weighed down, much heavier than she remembers.

Anna opens one eye. There is rich colour in her world again. She feels sticky with fresh blood.

She feels as if she has woken from a deep and dreadful nightmare.

That place was terrifying.

"Oh," she gasps. Her chest wound is wicked, wretched. The pain is immense. There is a dull thudding inside her head, and she longs to be sick.

Yet for a moment, she could fly. She did it. She was free, in an unknown place and it felt completely natural until that thing appeared.

The group, her family, was right to choose her as the fifth. She was born unwanted, yes, but she was also born to soar.

Hearts do not need to stop in order to astral travel, the anchor that binds really can stretch.

From the corner of the room, Alex steps out of the darkness and gloom.

She gasps and braces herself for the fury he is sure to have. Forbidden realms and broken rules.

Oh shit, now what?

Instead of anger, he claps slowly.

"I knew you could do it, Anna. I knew it, we all did. You walked in another world."

His face shows excitement, and something else, pride.

Despite her pain, her guilt, and her fear, Anna smiles. She peeled back layers.

"I did," she gasps. "I really did."

*H*er wounds are tended to by Isabelle. Gently, and with such compassion, Anna wonders if a rule breaker like her even deserves the kindness shown. She is wrapped in a blanket and treated like a refugee from elsewhere, from a war-torn land.

She is led downstairs on shaking legs that can barely hold her and given a glass with a generous amount of her favorite whiskey inside.

Bethany orders food, pizza. It seems like such a routine and mundane act for such an extraordinary and life-changing event.

There is to be a special meeting inside Kingdom House, an announcement and celebration. Truly, for the first time, she is now one of them. Gifted, special, unique. Capable of astral travel, adept at leaving her body. She's proven herself and it won't ever be so hard again or so wretched. From now on, hallucinogens will aid her, and ritual pain will be the rocket fuel to send her flying.

Her true family is proud of her, even after her disregard for the rules.

Glory is hers and yet it isn't. The figure she saw greatly disturbed her. She can't shake the image out of her mind.

Why was it, did it hate me?

To it, everything was its enemy, all was its nemesis but there was an odd kind of beauty too. It was glorious.

Did it say something to me?

The encounter is still jagged in her thoughts and memory, a storm that won't settle.

Together, clustered in a circle, the group of five sit. Loud and exciting conversations are happening around her, and she struggles to keep track and focus.

Isabelle laughs but Anna has missed the joke. Time jerks.

She feels lightheaded and weak. Neither thing helps her thick confusion and missing memory to straighten out.

Blood loss? She wonders. She needs to rest and recover.

She will have to change the sheets on her bed and flip the mattress before she can sleep. She feels cold, weary, and exhausted all the way into her bones.

Yet exhilaration overcomes all.

I did it, it doesn't matter what I saw or what might have spoken, I did it.

The people around her are special and now she is too. They know the secrets of the universe or something close to it.

Hidden realms. New worlds to explore.

Purity in pain.

It was true, all of it.

What would humanity do if they collectively possessed the knowledge her group holds? If society knew as an absolute certainty that the end is not the end at all, but merely a natural change. A separation with the main essence, and with consciousness remaining intact. The body acting as little more than a home to occupy until it breaks down or fails.

Would people rejoice or reject? Would life become something that could be discarded easily, and thrown away?

Would other worlds be full of people searching endlessly or would it bring comfort to those who are swallowed by loss and grief?

Lost inside her own troubling thoughts, Anna fails to notice that Alex has stood up. He clears his throat, and the quick sound makes her jump.

"Pay attention, sleepy head," Bethany pokes her in the arm and whispers.

For a brief slice of time, Anna is disorientated, muddled in a way she can't explain.

Reality bleeds crimson.

She finally bled her way into a different realm and the cost was not death. Her vision briefly flashes to black and white.

She shakes her head. It must be blood loss, pain and whiskey, bad combinations.

"To Anna, our little rule breaker," Alex announces and raises his glass.

"To Anna," the group choruses.

This is in my honour! Me.

She has never felt so much love or received so much attention. She loves and feels loved. She is seen.

My true family. I belong here.

Whoever her birth parents were, they didn't want her. She was left near a group of bins, as if she were something to be thrown away, alone and newly born, with little chance of survival. Rubbish.

She was only discovered by chance, a passing person heard her cries and found her. But fate had cruelty in store.

The foster homes and children's homes she lived in were no place for any child. Abuse and acts of violence were all she came to know. She had no self-esteem, no respect for herself, and no real understanding of kindness.

She tried to trust and love her ex-boyfriend and best friend, one last attempt. Yet they discarded her too and only craved each other.

No one ever wanted her, or needed her, except for the people currently around her. Now she can live and thrive.

She understands she will do anything for any of them, within reason. They are hers and she is theirs.

"Tomorrow night," Alex continues. "At midnight, we will leave our bodies as one and travel further than ever before, together. Anna, I believe you are now ready to join us in our group astral exploration. The door we need requires the energy of five."

Tomorrow night?

Will she even have time to rest and prepare her fractured state?

What about the thing I saw, will it be there too?

"DMT and ritual will aid us, as we will help each other. We aim for a forbidden realm my father once saw. Divine beings inhabited a place of wonder. Questions can be asked, and answers received. Not the realm encountered during hallucinogenic trips, but one far above."

"The place he wrote about in his diary," Bethany confirms. "We go through The Void."

The Void?

"Our father spent a lifetime trying to access one particular doorway and he found a way with the instructions in the book that is now mine, sorry, ours I mean. This place, it's beyond the ones we know. Many levels higher."

He lets the words sink into the group clustered around him. Isabelle's eyes are wide and excited, a look Anna hasn't seen her wear before. Matt is smirking and Bethany appears in awe. How similar they all look, how closely they resemble each other, how odd it is.

"The entities inside this realm are all-knowing. So, essentially, prepare your questions," Alex continues. "And may you receive the answers you desire."

Anna has a question. Why, why must there be so much separation and suffering in the world, in reality?

Humanity has never been so corrupt or divided.

Why is such true occult knowledge hidden from the population? Choices are removed and kept secret, away from human eyes. People are not given the opportunity to learn about life-changing subjects when they don't know such information even exists.

Surely there would be no separation in the world if everyone understood they were all one, and all equal. The body is a temporary home for spirit, the soul is all power.

An answer could change me too, heal me. If I went through so much for a reason, it might make all the difference to who I am.

She can admit she is still broken inside and doubts she can ever be whole. Flesh scars heal, emotional wounds rot and fester. Once something is broken, a person can always sense the cracks and weak parts. Her fury too, her fierce anger towards injustice and those who hurt her in her past, the unfairness of life. Is her constant inner rage something that could be cast aside and left behind?

"Anna?"

"Oh, I'm sorry. What did you say?"

"I asked if you could tell us what you saw."

The curious feeling of deja-vu swarms her.

She thinks back to that first night in the empty pub that looked so derelict on the outside.

Tell us what you saw.

The sensation makes her head spin. Silence descends. She coughs, just for something to hear.

"Perhaps Anna is tired," Bethany suggests. "We should eat and sleep, so we'll be well rested."

Alex ignores his sister.

"Anna," he prompts. "Tell us."

The man knows how to apply pressure while still appearing polite and gentle. She broke the rules, and now the least she can do is share her experience.

"Okay, I was desperate," she begins. "It was my last chance to prove myself. I pushed my body to the absolute limits of pain, and it worked, the training and meditation kicked in, I think. I rose up and out, well, it was more of a stumble really. But there was a different world, like the one I saw when I died but at the same time, I sensed it was very different, then again, it wasn't. I…"

She stops, aware that chills have crept across her body. The whiskey churns in her system and works to numb the viciousness of her chest wound.

"I…I saw this house and I had the cord, the silver cord you all talked about. I saw something else too."

"What?" Bethany asks, intrigued.

"A huge creature first, it was just swimming in the sky, minding its own business. And then there was a white owl and a figure, a being. There was a noise like a trumpet only deeper and I think I know what made the sound, it was the being, the entity. It was dark and made of charred flesh."

"Made of what?" Isabelle asks, astounded.

"Charred flesh and lined with little sharp fins like a shark has. I know how this sounds, but I sensed it, it was evil and beautiful too, kind of. It spoke, I think, only…"

"It spoke?" Isabelle echoes and half shrieks.

"Yes, it spoke to me, in my mind. Did I go lower again, does anyone know because I don't want to go back there again. Ever."

Alex sits down, seemingly deep in thought. She looks to him for answers. He was once like her, a student too. He studied under the ways of his father and learned everything at the feet of him.

"A charred being?" He questions.

"Yes. It was terrifying. She had bright blue eyes."

"She?"

"Yes, I think so."

"I see."

Does he?

Dark shadows cross his face. Anna can't read his expression.

"Anna, we've never seen anything like that. At least, not where we've been, and we've travelled to many realms. Entities exist in special places only and only five can reach them."

This time it is Bethany that speaks.

"Oh."

"What did this charred being say to you?"

I can't recall.

The knowledge she needs is on the very tip of her tongue, the outer limit of awareness. She closes her eyes, concentrates and conjures the memory more easily than she expected. Those sharp fins, its difference, its defiance, its power, its need.

What did it say? Reveal? No, wait, I remember! Revenge.

"I…"

She stops. Something feels off, the curious extra sense she possesses warns her to remain silent.

"I forgot, I'm sorry," she lies.

The doorbell rings and saves her from the spotlight she fears.

"Pizza's here!" Bethany squeals and claps her hands.

The heavy atmosphere of the room lifts instantly, she can feel turmoil leave. She stares at Alex briefly, he doesn't look happy anymore, he looks deep in thought, troubled or apprehensive.

He looks up, catches her staring, and offers her a weak smile. He is disturbed, she can sense it. His eyes narrow with suspicion.

"Alex," she begins. "I did see it, I honestly did."

"Ok. I believe you. What did it say to you, have you truly forgotten?"

Revenge. That's what it said.

"I'm sorry, I really don't recall," she answers.

"You must have more natural skill than I guessed. It takes years for people to encounter such beings during astral travels and have breakthrough experiences."

"Oh."

"Well, let's just see where tomorrow takes us, shall we?"

Maybe he doesn't know which realm I went to?

Alex claims his father was an absolute expert, and now he owns the information the man once possessed. She only knows that according to him; all possibilities are alive and exist. Astral projection lets a person slide into the nearest universe in ordinary circumstances. Rituals work as a map, a stargate, a tunnel to elsewhere forms from intention.

It doesn't make any real sense.

Anna is missing something, and she knows it, still, another out-of-body journey feels too soon.

"I don't know, Alex. Are you sure it isn't too much for me? I don't want to go back to that place."

"You won't. You'll be with us. The ritual sets our location, remember? It binds us together and once something is loose; it never becomes firm again. There is no anchor, no chain. Do you understand that?"

"I think so."

It's always odd to figure out the metaphorical ways of Alex.

"We'll all be fine, have faith, Anna. I'll look after you."

"Do you promise?"

"Yes, I do."

Trust. Every time she placed her trust in others, they smashed her feelings to pieces and stamped on the remains. Yet that doesn't mean everyone is the same, doesn't mean everyone will let her down, does it?

Not all of society and the people in it are identical, not all are bad or rotten at the core.

Alex, Bethany, Isabelle, and Matt, none of them have hurt her so far. They've shown her nothing but kindness and compassion, friendship and love. Besides, Matt is new to the group and he's fine and safe, indifferent yes but happily so.

"Okay," she eventually says. "Okay, I trust you."

She knows she should feel grateful and excited, she will travel on the ultimate journey with people who care for her. She will not be in any danger. So why does apprehension grip her so tightly?

Why is her instinct screaming and why is she afraid?

Revenge
What did it mean, revenge for what or against who?
Is something after her?

Anna wakes up in her clean bed, at least, a partly clean bed.

Her chest wound and thigh cut have been bleeding and weeping overnight. She makes a mental note to ask Isabelle for new dressings, although it is likely she needs stitches in her leg. The burn on her chest might become infected too if she isn't careful.

Burns.

Immediately she thinks of the charred figure and the way puffs of smoke spiraled away, as if it had just stepped out of a raging fire.

What was it really? It was so familiar.

How many bizarre landscapes and bleak realms are there and why must leaving her body require such extraordinary self-sacrifice? She wanted to find a way to become whole, not more torn.

Why does agony have to be the fuel to lift her?

Are they the first group to achieve such astral travels or have many come and gone before them, aside from The Kingdom House founder?

Alex and Bethany's father died in a car accident a year before her arrival and neither one seems to mourn his sudden passing or mention him with any regularity. Perhaps there is no grief to suffer when the end is not the end at all, only a new beginning. They claim they don't have any family photographs of him to display either.

There are so many questions I want to ask Alex, too many.

Maybe after tonight, she will get her chance.

She pushes the thoughts away and recalls her strange dreams instead. Dark, silver-colored oceans cascaded over red grains of sand; she can picture the images perfectly as expertly crafted paintings in her mind. There was a beach of some kind, lined with huge shimmering volcanoes with lilac lava spilling down. It was a quiet place, a place she could wander freely. Her feet made tracks in the curious sand and bat-like creatures flew overhead, unbothered by her. A perfectly shaped massive sphere, full of rainbow light hung in the sky, colours rippled with wild beauty and strange elegance inside. A pure white owl with a huge wingspan flew circles in the air, a remnant of the owl she saw in her out-of-body exploration.

Normally, nightmares assault her every sleeping moment, glimpses of past events she tries so desperately to forget. Her dream was a nice change of scenery.

Does it mean I'm healing? Now that I'm wanted and loved, now that I belong?

Either way, it's a pleasant way for her to wake up.

Are dreams other realities too?

She is not sure which world is the most vivid. Reality has become muddled and confused.

Endless realms of afterlife places, other dimensions, are they all the same or different?

Alex should know, but she's asked before and received no solid answers.

'I'll tell you when you're ready,' is the line he repeats so often or the overused, *'You'll see for yourself.'*

Dismissals.

She rubs her eyes, briefly seeing a kaleidoscope of brightness, and checks the time on the clock beside her. It is almost midday. No doubt the others are meditating and preparing for tonight.

She should be doing the same, but it was kind of them to let her sleep.

She sits up and pushes her hair off her face. Her brain thuds, her limbs ache and her self-inflicted injuries feel as vibrant as splashes of red on a white canvas.

Yet she has a lot to be happy about. She can stay in the house; she can be with the people she has come to need and admire.

What would her ex-fiancé and former best friend say if they could see her now? Her torn body, her lacerations, and her boney frame.

If they could gaze upon her, they would gasp in shock, horrified, riddled with fake concern but both would miss one essential thing. Her smile, her strange glow. She can walk in other worlds.

She is different, special and unique.

That day, that moment in the bookstore led to her profound rebirth. She took the path that led to redemption.

She truly is a phoenix bird, without the pile of ashes, and tonight, she will visit a new realm. The one they all talk of The Void.

They will travel together to the place with the doorways. She will never wander in terrible, frightening realms again, not when she has her group by her side.

Through her lessons and studies, she knows and understands that existence and reality are like that of an onion. Layer after layer form a sphere, the illusion of a solid state.

Human vision is restricted and unable to see the full light spectrum of realities. But a soul can.

The energy of five is needed to penetrate a further, higher place, according to Alex and his father's teachings.

She is the fifth and there will be no cords to bind them, the special ritual words will see to it.

She closes her eyes and gives herself a moment. What will the day bring?

Her life is different now, new days mean new things and happenings, surprises. There is no dread upon waking.

The mundane is obsolete, routine is gone. She stands uneasily and crosses to the window, briefly thinking of the night before, when the wall was no obstacle.

Atoms vibrating at set frequencies make an object solid. The knowledge feels peculiar and bizarre.

Human beings are born and spend their early lives being told what to learn and how to behave. Freedom is a myth, an illusion.

Information is hidden from view. Real opportunity is not stolen, it is not given in the first place. People are numbers, cattle, trapped in a system without escape. Dreams are extinguished, and hopes are tampered down. True knowledge does not exist without searching, without plummeting into chaos. People who think differently are mocked, laughed at, and whispered about. Individuality is never embraced or accepted.

But I know the real secrets.

Anna smiles, briefly engulfed with happiness, the feeling is a new sensation.

She sees her group practicing yoga on the lawn below, led by Bethany.

She is glad she's missed this part of the day, she hates yoga, *hates* it. She falls over and the others laugh and pick her up, rolling their eyes at her inelegant ways.

She counts three people, one is missing. Of course, Alex.

Where is he?

She treads softly across the room and listens to the house. There are no sounds.

She closes her eyes and tries to sense his presence, the pulse and vitality of his energy in her mind.

It's a trick she's used since her childhood, a way to know when an enemy lurked or approached. A tactic of survival she developed.

Everyone, she believes, has an extra sense. It works like a muscle, and she has exercised hers for many years.

The trouble is, people are told no such sense exists, and restrictions are placed upon them. Beliefs in psychic abilities are not encouraged and if anyone claims to have such a skill, they are laughed at or labelled a fraud, a con artist.

Villains exist in charge of society, villains so vile that they cannot see the depths of their own cruelty. Society follows blindly and fails to stop and think or ask questions that might lead to new and wild understandings.

A person needs to believe and accept in order to see the truth. An everyday individual is not given the opportunities she has been gifted.

Evolution.

Anna believes her small amount of extra power is natural, evolution taking the first step in advancing the mind of a human being. Maybe one day such psychic gifts will be accepted as normal, ordinary. But not now, not in her current time.

She stretches her mind and feels her way.

She has a small inkling that Alex is in his study room. He wouldn't normally be locked away until the late evening, but she is sure he is in there, his energy is humming and loud.

She crosses the landing and puts her ear against the door. Yes, she can hear the rustling of papers, the sigh that escapes his beautiful lips.

She knocks twice.

"Yes?"

"It's me, Anna. Do you want a coffee?"

"I'll come down."

"Okay."

Now she can sense frustration. Something is bothering him. What? She does not know.

He's probably nervous about tonight. All five of us. His entire life led to this day.

By all accounts, Alex has been journeying the forbidden worlds the longest, Bethany second.

Their father was a well-known occultist in his prime, a collector of unique and disturbing items.

Human skulls, items owned by black magicians, a rare diary written and owned by the blackest, darkest magician of all, Aleister Crowley. Old copies of the Lesser Key of Solomon, private notes written by Madame Blavatsky, the founder of Theosophy, and parchment papers detailing secret Kabbalah teachings.

He travelled the world and also journeyed to other realms and talked freely with frightening yet divine entities, or so he claimed.

Throughout history, many people have had similar experiences and yet each journey appears so vastly different.

Some people, she knows, travel to other countries in order to experience the Ayahuasca method, or to take Peyote. Or failing that option, they use the dark web to find the substance. Many, if not all, claim that consciousness travels to other realms for knowledge and understanding. Some repeated travelers encounter life and have conversations with enlightened beings, machine elves, and multiple interdimensional entities.

Such travels have been occurring for thousands of years or more in all beautiful cultures. Mainstream society labels such exploration hallucinations, images conjured up by imagination, and nothing more. Of course, the false explanation is swallowed by the masses.

Modern medicine calls near-death experiences more of the same.

Anna knows both statements are utterly wrong and naive, and Kingdom House has pushed the boundaries further than all science-based discoveries.

The most valuable item Alex's father owned is a leather-bound grimoire, a decaying book of old rituals and spells written in an ancient middle eastern language. The Hidden Fragments, written by a person who claimed to be a peeler of layers.

The strange book seems to be Alex's most treasured possession. No doubt he knows and understands each word by heart, yet he reads and studies the pages constantly. No one else is allowed to touch the special object.

The swirling symbols the group paint on their skin, the words they speak, and the pain they endure, are from instructions found within those yellowed parchment pages.

Old wisdom and forgotten knowledge of how to astral travel.

Anna finds the book unsettling, the torture-like, vulgar images, the strange beings with various animal heads, and the guttural words each person must speak. She believes Alex must be obsessed, but to what end?

He is more eager to astral further than anyone, more desperate to push the limits and reach far beyond.

The Void is their goal, a place said to contain weak spots, doors essentially. Membranes that can be accessed and utilized in order to travel further. How? How does it all work? She has no real idea.

Does Alex want to better his father? Or be better than everyone?

Neither idea would surprise her and many things he claims to know as sacred knowledge make very little sense. His rules are upside down, his ways, back to front and the group, including her, follow him blindly.

They rescued her from a life she hated, and gratitude has become her tight leash.

Yet she trusts them, she trusts the people around her, feelings she never thought she would ever have. In her relationship with her ex, she'd held back severely. She tried to be a people pleaser, eager to make others happy above her own needs. She liked what he liked and did what he wanted to do. Her own personality never developed or had the chance to shine. She was his shadow, his willing slave, playing a role she thought he wanted of her. The memory of her own submissiveness makes her shake with rage.

Growing up in foster homes, she was only a small child, neglected and quiet.

The only eyes that ever landed on her were those of men with the vilest of intentions and perversions.

Men she would find and tear to shreds with her bare hands if given the opportunity.

Now she feels like a woman of contradiction or a completely different person. Within her time in Kingdom House, she's learned almost every aspect of herself and cultured new traits.

The unwillingness to forgive remains but she is braver than she ever guessed, more resilient, and determined. She is capable of more than she ever imagined. There is a force, a power inside her still rising to the surface, she can feel it bubbling quietly, growing stealthily.

The quiet fury, the rage of injustice she had is still present, it ripples underneath her skin like boiling hot lava. A secret she keeps to herself. She cannot extinguish the heat and has no real desire to try.

She once read in one of her self-help books that forgiveness was the key to becoming a better and therefore, happier person.

Anna cannot forgive, nor forget those who ruined her, those who destroyed her hopes, took what they wanted and cast her aside. The grace she needs is lacking, the memories too persistent.

She threw the book in a bin, furious at the self-righteous person who dared to write such false sentiments.

Anger, she knows, is a natural defense mechanism and necessary for survival. Emotion is needed to face threats. Hers is tenfold and chained down inside.

As she stands at the locked door, the barrier blocking her and Alex, she wonders about his own illicit feelings and secrets.

His body is more scarred than her own. Thick angry red lines mark his back, as if a whip was used for punishment and lashings. He seeks pleasure in nothing and no one. While his sister Bethany is light, he is all darkness. He craves to see almighty presences and receive answers to questions he won't share.

She does not find Alex sexually attractive, or does she? He feels like the equivalent of a wild tiger, beautiful to look at, but deadly to touch.

Like him, like everyone, her thoughts are mainly on learning and exploration. She certainly feels tied to him, as if fate intervened and bound them both by sturdy knots. She would hate it if he wasn't in her life. Existence would have no real meaning. Reality would be cold and frozen once more.

Loyalty, that's what he asked me for.

She understands he has that from her and walks away.

She tells herself that some things are not her business, including any secrets or doubts he may have. He could have kicked her out for disobeying the rules and he hasn't. She owes him.

Whatever he needs she will give him, within reason.

As for the way he compels her, the way he smiles and makes her shiver, the way she feels whole near him, she dares not examine the true meaning.

***

Isabelle changes her chest dressings; the pain is so fierce that Anna thinks she may pass out or leave her body by accident.

She was given strong painkillers, but they seem to have had no real effect.

"Is it infected?" She gasps as Isabelle tells her to own her agony and to control it.

Alex wanders over and peers at her burn.

"I have something new to try tonight. I'm going out to fetch it, I'll be back soon," he says and winks.

"Okay," Isabelle answers flatly.

Anna briefly believes she can take no more. There are several levels of pain, barriers, and thresholds.

All pain but the bright clarity of agony is just ordinary savagery. In hurt, there is only one singular moment that is blindingly exquisite and verges on madness.

She is sacrificing her sanity, sometimes, it really does feel as if her mind is coming undone.

She questions where she is in her life.

She is safe, to a point.

She understands that astral projection carries its own severe risks but now she will be with the others, surely those risks are less? The danger must have passed, and her worse trials are over and behind her.

Truthfully, she is counting down the seconds until she gets to leave her body once more and see higher worlds in her natural state.

She feels clumsy and heavy, trapped and imprisoned within blood, flesh, and bone. Reality feels uncomfortable and heavy. She much prefers being light and free.

The sensation of flying high, nothing in her ordinary life will ever come close to. She has seen greatness and even the extraordinary sights present on earth, are nothing in comparison.

"Are you excited for tonight?" Isabelle asks.

She tears a dressing backed with silver open and places it on her wound.

"And no, it doesn't look infected yet," she adds.

Isabelle is a quiet mystery that likely cannot be solved.

At times, she is light and carefree like Bethany. She is a mother hen to the group, dishing out advice and generally making sure everyone is emotionally sound. On occasion, she has a vague, secretive expression that looks very similar to the one Alex wears. Her face is lined and her body, like everyone, is heavily marked.

Yet Anna has no idea of who she really is, how old she is, or what her past might be.

There are surface people who choose not to share their history, an onlooker will only ever see what the person needs them to see.

Isabelle has full control of herself, her mask never slips. Although darkness does appear in her eyes on occasion, as if a storm of wild proportions is brewing.

She seems close to Matt, who is plain and lacks any real characteristics. All Anna knows is that he was a businessman of some kind or maybe he still is. She has no idea of how Isabelle or Matt even met Alex and Bethany.

"I asked if you're excited," Isabelle repeats.

"Oh yes," Anna replies dreamily. "I want to see the true void. Not the bad place again."

"You must have slipped through the cracks."

"I did?"

What does that even mean?

"Anyway, the Void is beautiful, it really is something else."

"You've seen it before?" Anna asks, intrigued.

"Yes, it's a vortex of all manner of curious things. Any and all possibilities. A gateway of sorts."

"Are there really intelligent beings? People I mean."

"They're not people. Entities exist in the next level up, which is where we travel tonight. I've seen glimpses before; they are glorious Anna. I crave nothing more than to see them again. They have the presence of mighty old gods."

At this, Anna feels her eyes widen, all pain is forgotten.

She lies back and wonders who or what these beings actually are. She imagines they must be magnificent, beautiful, and wise. The opposite of the thing she saw.

Do they care that humans wander into their world, or do they welcome the intrusion with love and peace in their hearts?

So, the group has seen The Void before. When?

"How long have you been here Isabelle, in this house I mean?"

"Many years. Relax, you're very tense."

"Sorry, I'm nervous. Afraid, a bit. I worry it's too soon."

"Don't be. We need you, Anna. You're plenty gifted enough. That's why you're our fifth. We'll keep you safe."

Have they never tried to find a fifth person before?

"Have you…"

"Anyway, hush, try to sleep," Isabelle interrupts her next question. "Tonight, is a big night. I'll fetch herbs from the garden, they'll help keep infection away."

"I'll go," she offers. "I could do with some air."

She knows the answer will be no. No one else is allowed near Isabelle's vast vegetable garden, the land she claimed as her own strictly private area.

As predicted, Isabelle shakes her head.

"No, you sleep. Go and rest."

"Okay."

They really are very kind to me.

How nice it feels to be so looked after.

Anna heads upstairs, she enjoys a long shower, the heat working wonders on her sore limbs and heavy worries.

She climbs into bed and drifts away, back into a dream world. There are no nightmares this time, she has two powerful weapons inside her dreams.

Hope and trust.

*I*t's dark when she wakes, almost pitch black. Immediately, her stomach rumbles. She cannot recall her dreams or when she last ate something. But Alex insists on fasting before astral projection, for purification purposes.

The pizza?

It feels like a lifetime ago and she only had one slice on account of the pain she was in.

Fresh nerves swarm, and butterflies of great magnitude flutter in the pit of her stomach. The sudden realization makes her breathless.

I'm not ready for tonight.

The brutal understanding hits. She is afraid and frightened of seeing the realm she visited before.

What if I slip through the cracks again?

It all feels too soon, too rushed, and chaotic. She needs time to absorb what

87

happened, time to think and reach her own understanding of events. She needs complete reassurance that she will reach a higher place.

The feeling she is missing some vital piece of information strikes her.

If life is but a dream, if life is a theatre, what is happening behind the scenes?

Calm down, everything is fine.

Isn't it?

· Trust might be fragile and easy to catch but hard to keep hold of.

She sits up and cries out as new waves of pain assault her. She reaches for two painkillers and swallows them greedily.

Now wait, let them work before I move.

The delay might give her a chance to straighten her thoughts from tangled into order.

"You're awake."

The darkness of her room forms the outline, the shape of Alex. Anna has no idea why he feels the need to sneak into her room. It's his house, but still. Does he enjoy watching her sleep?

Finding him there seems like an ordinary occurrence and half expected.

"Yes," she answers the obvious question.

Tell him. Explain. I'm stronger now. He'll understand my doubts.

88

"Alex, listen, I'm having second thoughts," she half whispers.

"About?"

"Tonight, it's too soon for me, I think. At least, I feel it's too soon. Can we delay it?"

"I wouldn't insist we go if I believed you couldn't handle it."

"I know, but…"

I can't let them down; they've never let me down.

The time is 10 PM. She has two hours to think and organise her mind. Alex said the ritual must begin at exactly midnight.

"Tonight, there is an extraordinary planetary alignment we can take advantage of. The energy of the solar system will help us to aim higher. The power in our sails so to speak."

What! How?

Anna doesn't believe in astrology or planets in conjunction with anything. Surely the vast and pretty spheres are too far away to cause any effects or have influence.

His words sound naive, a children's fantasy story.

But surely, he must know what he's talking about, he had his father and the book. Everything else he claimed was actually true.

Alex stands, crosses to her bed, and sits down beside her. She immediately senses his turmoil; she can feel a conflict of emotions roll off him. But why? She assumed he would be excited. Is he worried or unsure? She can't tell.

"Anna," he says. "You should trust me. I wouldn't let anything bad happen to you. I care about you, a lot I mean."

He's right, I should try harder to trust him.

Kingdom house is her salvation and not her downfall.

She holds her breath and dares not speak. Electricity swarms the room and threatens to spark.

Something is wrong with him. He feels different.

Her heart begins to beat erratically. He places a hand on her arm and rubs her flesh, finding every scar and rough piece.

"Anna," he repeats.

Why such thick despair? She can feel the fire, the uncertainty inside him. Choices and confusion, rich desperation and yet excitement underneath?

Blood, he's thinking of blood?

The sudden vision, a thought stolen from his mind, fills her own thoughts.

"What's wrong Alex, what's…"

But his mouth is suddenly on hers, his hands are wrapped in her hair. His tongue parts her lips and she is pushed down onto her bed, his weight pressing down on top of her.

While her mind reels in shock and violently rejects his touch. Her body responds with heat and fire. Her arms snake around him as he pushes her nightdress up and angles her legs apart.

This can't happen, this shouldn't happen.

But she can't stop, won't stop. Her body needs his, she understands her mind does too.

Friend, teacher, master, family. He is everything to her and now he is more. Lost in passion, lost in the touch of someone who knows her and still craves her, still wants her, she becomes primal in her need and desire.

His jeans are off, and he is pushing his way inside her roughly. There is no gentleness. He stifles her cry with his hand and moans with bliss.

The walls of the house could fall, and she would not know the disaster, would not be aware. All she can see and feel is him. All she knows is him.

Alex, Alex, Alex.

Love. How could she not know, not understand? Of course, she loves him. The moment she saw him she loved him. He saved her.

He growls her name, over and over, grips her hand, and cries out.

Fireworks of magic erupt inside her mind, pleasure reaches a climax, and she is carried away, briefly lost in her own euphoria.

He only lies still for a few moments. His body is slick with perspiration. Anna lays across his chest, trying hard to breathe evenly and to let what just happened sink in. The suddenness, the way it began so quickly. She never expected such a thing, never thought he saw her that way, as a woman.

They made love.

It wasn't an empty meaningless encounter. But the opposite.

Does it mean he loves her the way she now understands she loves him?

"I have to get things ready," he whispers.

"Okay."

"Do you feel braver now, brave enough to go ahead I mean?"

Anna searches around inside herself. Yes, her worries are less, and the fire of uncertainty and fear has been dampened. Alex has made his feelings known and it changes everything. Any doubts she had are now obsolete, vanished.

"Yes."

"Great. We'll talk about this, about what happened another time. Tomorrow maybe, but not tonight."

"Okay, but… did it mean something to you?"

"Anna, yes, of course."

He sounds utterly sincere.

Joy rises, and she smiles a smile only the darkness can witness.

She kisses his chest in reply. Alex dresses quickly and sneaks out of the room as if they are teenagers in a house of parents.

She is glad of the few minutes alone. She wonders if she could float to the ceiling with sheer happiness.

Love, she feels, is the most significant force any universe ever knew. She giggles softly.

What just happened? Does he love me

Although she feels adored and happy, the events of the last couple of days still feel too much to bear. She needs time to think and accept the quick changes.

She understands that she has secrets she even keeps from herself.

This is unbelievable and perfect, beautiful.

Anna, it seems, has a solid future but the house of Kingdom is not meant to be sexual. She knew that from the very beginning. Sex is never spoken of, never acted upon as far as she knows.

There are finer pleasures. That's what Alex always said. Finer pleasures in higher realms.

Now it looks as if she is not the only one who likes to break the rules.

***

She showers quickly and wanders downstairs. Half embarrassed, afraid to see if anyone knows or senses what just happened. She feels her expression might give both her and Alex away.

There is no one inside the main living room. The emptiness feels striking and hollow. Lifelessness, with only an old clock ticking on the wall, counting as always. Wait, no. She can hear mumbling. She listens carefully and follows the sound of voices.

Alex, Bethany, Matt, and Isabelle are all in the kitchen, clustered around a worktop like a small coven brewing trouble or magic, toil and trouble.

There is a curious, horrible scent in the air and pretty China cups are lined up in a row.

"Sleeping beauty awakens!" Alex smiles.

She follows his lead and decides she will also pretend. She knows how to act; the majority of her life has been a theatre.

"Are you feeling better?" Bethany asks as she spots her. "You look better."

"I think so," Anna says, aware for the first time that the atmosphere is heavy.

The scene feels out of sync somehow, as if she walked in on secrets being exchanged.

Paranoia, that's all.

How many times has she believed others were talking about her only to find out she was wrong? Imaginary persecutions have been her undoing several times before.

Besides, everything has changed now. Her doubts are silent because of Alex, her courage and determination are rushing to the surface.

I belong here. I belong with them.

"We're almost ready," Alex smiles. "We were about to wake you. It's nearly time."

Anna tries to catch his eye and fails.

Another time, he said. Not now.

Tonight is too important, of course, she should have faith and go ahead. Alex has proven he cares for her.

There are steel pins in wrappings sitting on the draining board. Strange, dried leaves too and a paintbrush stained with red and black swirls.

She fills a glass with water and drinks it steadily.

Everything is okay, I'll be fine, we'll all be fine.

"Come on Anna," Alex is beside her. He takes her hand and pulls her. His touch feels different. If they were bound before, they are now glued.

They walk along the long hallway into the dining room, which is never used as a dining room at all. When they eat, they use the living room and sit on floor cushions or group together at the kitchen table.

The dining room floor is bare, elegant Persian rugs have been moved and rolled up, away, and out of sight. Painted on the wooden floor is a huge symbol in red that makes Anna feel uncomfortable just by looking at it. How strange it seems, how serious and marked with intent.

It appears to be a five-pointed star, caught inside the shape of a trapezium, and yet it isn't, not quite. It has real dimension and depth.

Lines have been crisscrossed throughout and lead off into nowhere. Around the edge of a massive circle are more symbols. Sigils.

Ordinarily, they only use the images for protection, written and painted across their own bodies. It looks as if fresh paint has been added over the old paint of the very same design.

"This is the power source," Alex tells her. "It'll be as if we're plugged into the mains. This is true ancient magic."

"Oh."

"Take a seat."

He points to one of the symbols and winks.

The wink feels like a small acknowledgment of what happened between them. She smiles coyly, both pleased and relieved.

Four symbols are exactly the same, with intricate writings on each one. Hers is different and she pauses.

"Why doesn't mine match yours?" She asks. "And everyone else's?"

"Because you're new to this, that's all."

"Oh, okay."

She sits down cross-legged and makes herself comfortable. Her nerves begin to resurface. The ritual feels extremely serious, the equivalent of sitting an exam she hasn't once studied for.

The others walk in and take their places, all sitting on their own matching design.

Bethany, dressed in a white gown, appears serene and happy. Isabelle looks serious yet her eyes sparkle with excitement. Matt has no real expression, only a kind of grim acceptance.

I'm the fifth. Me.

She never imagined she would ever find herself in such a situation. She wonders if the group really is a cult and finds she doesn't mind.

Is a cult still a cult if the charismatic leader and his followers are correct?

Yet it is an odd place to find herself in, only three years before she was trying hard to end her life and now, she only wants to live a more vibrant existence than most.

Her quest for knowledge never ceases.

She looks at Alex, his eyes are closed as if he is having one last conversation with himself, one last run-through.

This is the most serious night of their lives.

Shouldn't it be hers too? She is sitting in a giant painted symbol, about to take hallucinogenic substances and cause herself agony.

It all feels utterly surreal, absurd, a place she never guessed she would be.

How did I get here?

From obscurity to the fantastic.

She watches as Bethany jumps to her feet and lights candles, there are five of them spread around the room, thick white pillar candles. She picks up a small tub, filled with lilac paint and dances toward Isabelle.

On the older woman's forehead, in the centre, she paints a symbol with her finger, a simple drawing that looks just like an owl.

The feeling of Deja-vu engulfs her and she knows it must mean something.

I saw an owl in my dreams and out-of-body travel. A beautiful white owl.

Bethany repeats the process with Matt, who sits calmly and smiles. She skips lightly and paints the very same symbol on the forehead of Alex.

"Why an owl?" Anna asks as soon as it is her turn.

"They represent wisdom according to the book," Bethany whispers. "May the divine give us high knowledge."

"Do owls walk in two worlds like us? Or fly, I suppose."

"No silly."

The paintbrush tickles her forehead, and she fights the urge to sneeze.

Knowledge. Why are we here, what are we and why?

Those are the questions Anna intends to ask.

Bethany presses play on an archaic tape machine that is sitting lonely and dust-covered in the corner. A strange tone immediately fills the room. Anna can feel the sound inside the marrow of her bones.

Special hertz frequencies, she knows, help the veil between realms to open. Still, it sounds like an obscure noise that hurts her teeth, a giant humming one note.

Bethany switches the main light off and takes her place, clapping her hands twice with glee.

"To new worlds!" She laughs. "And conversations with gods."

Anna smiles, she likes her enthusiasm a great deal, it's infectious, but she begins to feel odd.

Quite abruptly, the situation changes. Her hidden instinct, the small skill she came to depend on as a child, bursts into life like a fierce wildfire.

Danger is present, and chaos is close and bearing down upon her. Sudden pressure rests upon her, the weight feels like a titanium blanket interlaced with heavy dread.

A wave of dizziness cascades until she sways where she sits.

Something is very wrong.

"I feel a little…a bit strange," she says.

"It's the power in this room," Bethany grins. "Isn't it wonderful? The symbols work as actual signals too. The universe is watching us."

No. It isn't wonderful.

Everything feels wrong and upside down. The urge to run strikes her until her rational mind kicks in.

Calm down, I trust them. I'm okay. Trust.

One deep breath, two. She tries to centre herself. Last-minute nerves are ordinary and expected. She mustn't panic and ruin things for the others, for Alex.

Everything is happening too fast, there is no time to stop and think to absorb events.

This is all too much too soon.

Breathe, I'm okay. I'm safe.

But what if…

Before she can follow the thought, a China cup gets placed in her hands. The substance inside is dark and smells horrific.

"Psilocybin," Alex announces. "It tastes vile but it's the grease that helps unlock the door. Magic mushrooms in other words."

Anna closes her eyes. Yes, she knows the facts. Shamans, psychics, and even some remote viewers have used plants and mushrooms for countless years to access other realms, free consciousness, and move through time and space.

"I thought we were taking DMT?" She says.

"No, this is much better. It's purer. Everyone, listen please."

Stop this, run. Run away.

Anna does not move. A bead of sweat trickles down her spine and makes her flinch.

Alex sits down, clears his throat, and crosses his legs. His precious book rests in front of him, open in the middle.

Shadows play on the plain walls and create Picasso-style images.

Anna feels the wild urge to burn the dreadful book, she wonders if it would scream should flames touch the thick parchment.

"There is danger in what we do. Some realms and worlds are not meant for us, and we dare tread them anyway. We are true explorers. Adventurers. Soon, we will astral project further than anyone ever has and return safely.

Others visit one or two realms; we see and experience all."

From beside him, he removes a clear bag full of long and thick metallic pins. They look like the kinds used to pierce body parts for jewelry.

"Pain is purity. You are trained in body and spirit. At that heightened moment of suffering, free yourself. Let the chains fall away. Let your soul fly, let your energy become your true natural state. Focus on the words, they will take us where we need to go. You will not have cords, remember this. Now, drink."

Heaven's gate comes to mind, the Jonestown massacre. People, human beings brainwashed by a leader they have unwavering faith in and killed.

Is this poison?

Something is extremely wrong; she can feel it.

Stop, it's only paranoia.

Suspicious natures exists in those hurt; she isn't to blame for the way she is.

No one is going to poison me, I'm being stupid.

She is utterly torn, wretched with worry.

Anna watches the others and doesn't move. Bethany, Matt, and Isabelle drink their rancid tea in one go, although all gag loudly. No one drops down dead or starts to choke.

"Anna," Alex prompts.

Two paths face her, only one will lead to regret.

Warning bells are still sounding, fire is raging inside her mind, but the others around her are her family, her friends. They gave her a chance at a new life, a brand-new existence. They saved her and Alex made love to her. They haven't once hurt her or even tried.

She is someone now, not just another anonymous face in a packed crowd.

She is special, loved, and wanted. She belongs.

Trust them, drink it.

Yes, she's taken multiple drugs before but never a hallucinogenic substance.

What if I'm allergic, what if I have a bad reaction?

"Anna, trust me, please."

Her eyes meet his and she sees nothing but kindness and concern.

"It's safe," Alex soothes her. "I swear it."

He promises. Drink it. I mustn't let them down.

She nods once and knocks the drink back in one go. It tastes rotten, like raw sewage, and almost comes back up, she holds the bitter substance down and sweats profusely. Her eyes fill with tears and drip down her face.

"I'll follow you," Alex says and places his own full drink beside him.

Bethany begins a focused meditation, while Alex starts to chant his words of power. She knows the guttural vowels and words by heart and finds herself joining in, her lips moving automatically.

Minutes pass.

"The door," Bethany speaks. "Picture the veil shifting, the curtain between worlds opening, just for us. Concentrate."

Anna tries her absolute hardest.

Nothing is happening. I can't feel anything from the hallucinogenic.

No sooner does she think the words than reality begins to bend and fold.

As the chanting of their special words reaches a peak, a crescendo, the room begins to tilt like the spinning tunnel of a fairground ride.

An observer lurks near, she can feel tendrils of unlimited power wrapping around her.

It only takes a few minutes before Anna is sure she can sense a heartbeat in colours. Shapes appear in her mind, fractal designs of sheer mathematical structure.

Words are being born, and spilling from the mouth of Alex, she can see the letters falling.

A huge letter G comes tumbling off his tongue and lands on the floor. It grows tiny legs and scuttles off to hide in the skirting board. A letter U quickly follows.

She watches, amused, transfixed.

Somewhere far off, she believes she can hear drums, tribal drums, or an echo of history. She can't decide if the sound is her heartbeat or noise from the forgotten past. The air itself is shimmering like liquid, glowing and throbbing with a steady pulse.

The wooden floor beneath her becomes soft and pliable. She giggles loudly and wonders who made such a strange sound.

Laughter, what an odd thing.

Why does humour exist? What makes something funny and why do human beings make such an absurd sound that is often so infectious?

For a brief slice of time, Anna thinks she knows the answer, but it flashes away, out of reach.

She is no longer afraid, only tired.

She wants her body to sleep while she flies to the edge of everything. Mysteries need to be uncovered and dragged kicking and screaming into the light. She has questions. Answers may change her life further.

I went swimming in the air. I left my body.

"I can fly," she mumbles.

"Yes, yes you can, Anna."

Anna. That's me.

Alex is in front of her, crouching like the wild cat he is. She didn't see him move. He has a glowing halo of swirling red, colours of deep anger.

"Concentrate now, pain is purity, take it and use it. Now, lay back. Be calm."

Her vision is distorted, all she can see is him. He *is* darkness, she was right, she can see it inside him, pulsing like a black and rotten heart. Is it too late to change her mind, too late to run?

He cradles her head as she lays down.

He lifts her skirt.

His actions feel sexual, and she becomes confused. Are they making love again right now? Astral projection transcends human pleasures, he said so.

His hands are on her thigh. He pinches roughly and now she knows, realizes.

He aims to hurt her and release her so she can soar and make friends with the clouds.

"Find the others," he whispers. "You must find them, Anna."

Yes, I will.

She tries to speak her thoughts and only incoherent mumbles escape her lips.

Alex forces the thick surgical pin through her pinched skin. Explosions burst inside her mind. She arches her back in blinding pain, still anchored to her body, and screams.

The agony in her chest fades as the pain in her thigh increases and still, it is not enough. Why is it never enough?

Alex twists the pin with fierce brutality and now she jerks in turmoil. That heightened moment of clarifying agony beyond belief hurtles towards her. She grabs it with both hands.

Anna comes loose. She is free.

*T*here is no grey replica house this time. No room or echo, no shadow or shade. The walls vanish and Anna's soul, her consciousness, takes flight and speeds through a tunnel, a vortex far above.

Alex promised and he was correct, she was right to force herself to have faith in him. Her trust was never an illusion.

True freedom.

She can be as ancient gods once were, an unstoppable force, a wild mystery without a solution, hot or cold, contradictions of indifference.

She has no recollection of closing her eyes or opening them. She feels her energy move at high speed, entrenched by primordial darkness until she pauses, and stops entirely.

Her vision slowly returns, and comes alive, from obsolete to impossible witness.

She assesses her surroundings.

There are fields full of tall and twisted purple sunflowers, each flower has sharp metallic spikes instead of the curved petals she is used to. An alien world of existence. Each stalk has drops of dark liquid leaking out and falling into rippling silver pools.

Endless miles of blackened, crooked trees follow. The barren and sinister landscape looks as if a fire tore through and left no life present. Mist sweeps the ground with tendrils spiraling outwards in soft curls.

She is standing on a bare and grey track of geometric shapes. Although she has no solid feet to speak of, she can feel the hard and rough ground beneath the force that is her.

Above is a sky of deep undulating crimson shades, pitted with stars set in curious, perfectly straight lines of strict order.

Where am I?

Multiverse, universe, layers, hidden realms. A million or more choices.

The Void. Endless in-depth and far-reaching in consequence. Yet there must be some mistake. Her cord, her tether, she still has it.

She takes hold of the thin line of energy in confusion, the other end snakes off into places unseen. It feels hot and is pulsing rapidly, she can feel the hum, the power it contains.

As she watches, it begins to fall apart, disintegrating until it falls like a shower of pretty confetti-like glitter. The sparks hit the ground and settle as a collection of dull pinprick lights.

The ritual must have worked.

The ground reacts and vibrates beneath her. The remains of her cord, the particles of glitter, are glowing and changing. Each one rapidly explodes to the size of a coin. Multiple, coarse and spiky limbs burst out, bringing the sparks to life with a resounding popping noise.

She steps back, instantly afraid. The tiny new, spider-like creatures scuttle away at speed, chittering wildly as they flee.

What are they, and what is this place?

She feels just as Alice did when she chased a white rabbit and tumbled down into wonderland.

For a moment, Anna wonders if the experience is happening inside her mind only, a hallucinogenic trip, her imagination on fire with insane ideas and nothing more.

No, this is real.

She touches her human-shaped energy and sees the reaction, the ripple, and feels the sensation.

This is truly happening.

110

The world she stands in is more alive than her own.

Her tether is gone, she has no restriction now. Anna searches behind her, she is the only light within sight.

Where are my friends and Alex?

If ritual sets the destination, they must be close.

Should she walk or fly to search for them? Fly, of course. She wills herself to rise and finds she can't. A superhero with all powers lost.

"Hello?" She calls out and her voice only echoes with emptiness.

There is no one with her. No Alex or any of them.

She knows it is important not to panic, she will find her way, she's been lost many times before.

A quick sound erupts behind her, a loud yap that doesn't seem to belong in the realm she stands in.

She turns, surprised, and sees a silver mechanical clockwork dog making its way across the track. That dog is intricate, with carved symbols as decoration, symbols not unlike the ones usually painted on her physical body.

She can see a large key in its back, rusty and turning in slow, creaking circles.

What the…

How could such an earthly toy exist inside the Void and how did it get here? She watches, transfixed by the strange sight. The dog moves on, oblivious to her, jumping away in awkward jerking movements.

I need to go. I need to find them.

Has she arrived in a different realm to the one her friends are in?

Overhead, a huge white owl flies in complete silence. It looks so enigmatic and graceful, familiar too. Is it a sign?

"Wisdom," she whispers.

Follow it.

She moves just one step forward, and the ground cracks beneath her. Anna can see black lava moving in a fast stream of bubbles and steaming heat. It looks like hot tar.

She runs.

She is pure energy fleeing, light and translucent but grounded. An explorer of forbidden territory, a stranger in a new land racing away at speed.

Above her head, the sky cracks open with a high-pitched wail. An earthquake in reverse. A jagged chasm appears, the inside is filled with burning lilac twists and violent black shadows that swoop in elegant motions, caught in a dance of their own design. Around the edges are sharp crystals clustered together. Impossible sights.

112

An amethyst sky. A primordial vision, a view of life beyond the stars.

For a moment, she stops, transfixed by the strange and hypnotic beauty the sight holds. It is mesmerizing, full of depth and wonder, the equivalent of watching the birth of a new universe.

A heartbeat of power exists around her, a force of endless potential caught without harmony.

But she can't stand and stare at new and glorious, magical things, she has to find the others.

Where are they?

The Void is vast, endless, with no true beginning and no end.

She hears that sound again. The bellow, the trumpet. It is low and fierce and carries with it the promise of significant threats.

The noise comes from above and below, from each side until it feels loud enough to cause her madness with its wild ricochet.

What is that?

It is a warning, a call to arms, she knows this, feels the knowledge. Feelings are how the multiverse is talking to her, and how she is navigating. Her curious environment turns cold.

She veers off into the fields of tall but rotten trees or some version of.

There is anti-life around her, a reverse of birth. Decay and rot, necrotic wastelands.

113

Thick nets, cobwebs in complicated patterns cover the tallest gnarled branches within sight, each strand ripples with dark energy. She speeds through, faster than imagination, eager to discover doorways or exits.

Soft bits, through which she can escape.

A crack in the ground faces her, a chasm, a drop-down into oblivion. She forces herself to stop at the very edge and peers down. Blood red fire swarms in tall, elegant motions, trapped inside the crimson flames are images of screaming human beings.

The violent sight makes her head fizz and pop.

People, burning and writhing in eternal agony. She is witnessing pure undiluted nightmares.

"I don't understand," she says. Her shock feels electric.

Where am I?

The thought that she may not even be close to the same world as her friends strikes and makes her stagger.

Anna needs to leave, needs to run away as far as she can get. How will such terror ever be erased from her thoughts? The visions of humans screaming have stained her eyelids like

114

the darkest of ink spills. She can taste the fear hanging in the atmosphere.

Should I help them?

Instinctively, she knows she cannot. Something is playing out in front of her, lessons that are incomprehensible. Pawns in something else's game, a plan she is no part of.

Do I wander until my body wakes up?

Anna does not know enough and has not been told vital information. Alex never once instructed her what to do if she ever found herself lost and stuck inside the boundaries of a strange and unknown world without her physical body close.

Stay calm, I'll find my group.

She follows the edge of a second chasm filled with stars until she sees a wooden building upside down. It appears to be similar in design to an earthly church, yet it is balancing precariously on its spire.

The sight is disorientating, she wonders if she might be the wrong way up instead.

Intrigued, she walks forward. The building is covered in thick rope-like tangled vines of dark green and black, each strand is infested with what appear to be open sores. It all looks old somehow and doesn't belong.

She wants to peer inside but knows she mustn't.

We're meant to be explorers.

She circles the building, looking for a way inside. There is a large, splintered crack, a way in that looks difficult and jagged. She pushes forward and enters a dark room.

How can I see when I have no eyes?

The concept rattles her and yet her vision does adjust with ease. The inside is not upside down and not empty either. Dark human figures sit on several lines of pews. They each looked draped in silver cloth. She counts, there are twenty of them, all sitting still.

At the place an altar should be, there stands a figure engulfed by vivid yellow fire. It waves its arms as if conducting an invisible orchestra and seems not to care that fire is eating it alive. Its mouth moves but she hears no sounds.

What is this building?

What kind of worship is taking place

As one, the congregation turns to stare at her. They each have blank faces under their hoods, without features. No eyes, nose, or mouth, only pale flesh. Human-shaped mannequins. Waxwork people unfinished.

For a brief moment, all she can do is gaze in shock until something touches her.

A thick green tentacle, lined with what looks like wet suction pads and sharp thorns, tries to wrap around her energy. She screams and lashes out, spins and darts away, back through the crack in the wall.

I hate this place! Am I inside someone else's nightmare?

Now what, how can she escape, find her body, and rejoin with her physical self? Is there some version of Kingdom House present somewhere?

That has to be the answer. Every lesson she was taught was about getting into new realms, slipping through doors that shouldn't exist. No lesson ever taught her how to leave if her body is not within reach.

She is too vulnerable alone.

Where are they?

The ground rumbles and undulates like a rug being shaken. The sudden force knocks her over. The sky suffers a quake and cracks with a resounding snap. A single bloodshot green eye appears and blinks once.

What is that!

It focuses on her and her alone. She can feel the hate it has. It views her with sheer loathing, intolerance.

Anna knows. The landscape is not for her, she should not be where she is. Surely it is an astral plane of lost things, of terrible wretched things?

True reality is incomprehensible and beyond human understanding. To even try is a path that leads only to madness. She is tiny, insignificant. A single drop in an unfathomable ocean. A mere pest against an almighty force of annihilation that has no name or need of any title.

Get away.

Anna runs, far away from the eye that stares with such violence and hunger. Into a patch of tangled gnarled trees, she flees, afraid.

This is all a mistake. I need to wake up. Please, real me, wake up!

She wonders if she could have followed her cord to find her way out, should it still exist. She was excited about the loss of her tether and now she wishes she had it once more. It wasn't to bind or prevent, it was to protect.

She sits and forces herself into a ball, an orb. Her inner fury is no use, no help, but what about her other gift, her extra sense?

She places a hand on the ground and clears her thoughts, feeling the way with her mind.

The Void is made from cruel ideas, and acts of twisted evil. Depravity. Lies and sins created the realm. The force of hate, corruption, and perversions fashioned the entire landscape. Energy never dies, it only changes state.

She is in a world of reverse and far away from goodness or light of any kind.

Power she can't truly understand ripples beneath the surface, malignancy festers in every part.

118

How do I get out?

The answer won't come or can't be comprehended. The knowledge is not for a human being.

I have to do something!

Quick movement catches her eye, and she sees the purest of horror. A figure walks by, oblivious to her. Its skin has been stripped away, only nerves, tendons and glistening muscles show.

The flesh of its legs have peeled away and collected around its ankles like a pair of baggy jeans. It stumbles and wanders, mumbling words she cannot catch. Its head turns and stark white eyeballs land on her.

"Help," it says, its voice hoarse and sore.

She sees its insanity, its pain, its desperation, and understands its plea for assistance.

No, it's a him.

What did the man do to deserve such a fate?

"Help," he repeats.

Anna stands quickly, her panic growing like a life force.

What can I do? Nothing.

She doesn't want to become involved with the peeled man with no flesh.

An image lands in her mind, she tries to force it away and out, but it settles like heavy fog. An older man, crouched over a wooden desk, with a feathered quill clutched tightly in his wrinkled hand. The sound of scratching on parchment paper, candles bright around him.

The Peeler of Layers.

The author of The Hidden Fragments.

If this is what became of him, what does it mean for her?

Did he become trapped somehow and now this is his eternal fate?

Leave.

She spins and runs, sprinting rapidly through a dark field, its bounty rotten and rancid, trying to think with clarity and not fear.

She searches frantically until a sole light in the far distance catches her attention.

Is that…

A singular bright light graced with blue edges. The light is acting as a beacon just for her.

Anna knows who it is, she senses such a thing. It is Bethany, glowing like a lighthouse and with her as the lost ship about to crash into unseen rocks.

I found them! They are here!

Joy erupts, excitement, and relief. Everything will be fine now; she was lost, that's all and now she's been found.

All that panic was for nothing.

They will journey together, as one. Her group must have been worried about her. She is their fifth after all, they need her, only five can open the door.

She heads straight for the light, across a bare road without purpose, thrumming with excitement, and stops. She rebounds sharply and hits the hard ground.

What happened?

She scrambles up, tries again, and fails.

A wall stands between her and Bethany, an invisible barrier that seems to be fiercely solid, utterly impenetrable. Confusion sparks inside.

I did something wrong! This must be my fault. I'm not where I'm meant to be.

"Bethany," she says. "What should I do? Help me. Tell me what to do."

Her words echo and bounce.

Alex said I was strong enough!

She places her hand against the wall, it feels cold, frozen like a thick sheet of Arctic ice. She pulls away and gasps.

What is happening? I don't understand.

She watches helplessly as three more lights, souls, begin as tiny sparks, flames, and flicker into existence. The four collect in a circle and quickly amass a human shape.

She knows each one, Alex, Bethany, Isabelle, and Matt.

Again, she hurries forward, eager to be with her group, her beloved family.

Still, the barrier remains. A complete separation, a curtain or veil she cannot penetrate.

Confusion, frustration, worry, and shock threaten to overwhelm her.

"It's me. Help me!" She cries.

Why isn't Alex doing anything?

"Help," she repeats.

She needs to tell them about the odd things she saw, the strange church and the frightening man, the Peeler of Layers.

Can they see me?

Yes.

One translucent figure steps towards her, the brightest, shining light. Alex. He is human-shaped like the others, like her, and more real, vibrant.

He'll help me, he'll know what to do.

She tries to tell him she can't reach the group and discovers her words are lost and stolen from her mouth before she can speak.

In the world she stands, in the forbidden realm, emotions are language, feelings and images are the real means of communication between life.

He holds out a hand, a single hand and she reaches out, desperation rising higher.

Palm flat, his actions mean stop.

What is he doing? Why is…

122

A sudden bombardment of images assaults her, memories of his, actions led by him.

Anna knows. Anna understands in one brutal blow.

No! Please no!

Her solid self falls and collects in a heap on the hard ground. Frozen shock spreads across her, far colder than liquid nitrogen, dead space inside.

She will not be travelling further. There is no exploration or exit for her, no door, and no way out.

Anna is dead.
Murdered.
Betrayed.
Sacrificed.
Trapped.

*T*he smooth blade of the ritual knife penetrated her chest only moments after she left her body. Alex wasted no time. The cold steel stopped her heart. Sharp metal versus a beating bloody organ. She had no chance to fight back, her body was vacant. She felt nothing of the cold metallic invasion.

Anna screams as her mind is poisoned, violated with scenes she will never remove.

How easily he killed her. How smoothly and without regrets, or sorrow. Her murder was clinical and cold, essential in his eyes. A sacrifice and she was no loss to him.

He never loved her; he never even liked her. None of them did. They each saw her as a thing they needed, not a person they wanted in their lives.

Alex slid the knife in deep and smiled, watching as her empty body buckled in protest.

Some part of her left behind still tried to fight but her death came swiftly. The sandglass that is her life is empty.

Trust, shattered.

Hope, not only broken but torn to shreds and swarmed by fire. Betrayal of the highest order.

She screams, lost in emotional turmoil.

After everything, the pain, the mutilation of her body, the faith she had, the love she felt.

How could they do this to me, how could Alex?

The knowledge will not sink in, she hardly dares believe the savage truth. Disbelief builds a wall to protect her.

It can't be true.

"Alex," she cries. "Bethany, please. This can't be. You wouldn't!"

Of course, they would.

She had it all wrong.

She was taken in, fooled, lured, compelled, manipulated, and used. Killed.

"WHY?" She wails.

The trumpet sound erupts behind her. Closer, nearer.

Fear, she can feel it infecting her soul. Her light inside is dying. Fade to black.

She thought Alex loved her, she thought they all did.

Beneath her, the ground begins to quake, something is coming. She needs her hidden rage but all she can feel is thick despair.

She spins and sees.

Darkness approaches, a thick blanket of. The blacker-than-black shape bears down at high speed. A whirlwind of bleak chaos.

Inherently she knows, it is coming for her.

She is a payment. The cost that pays the toll, the price to pay for opening a special, locked door. The fifth, her. She was marked for death from the beginning, chosen for killing.

Even chaos has strict order.

A butterfly flaps its wings in one world, a whirlwind begins in another.

Choosing her, teaching her, was all nothing but a sadistic game. She was always meant to die, and she had to walk into the strange world willingly and with love in her heart for the offering to work.

The blindfold around her eyes was tied by her own knots.

Fury begins to rise, fear, hatred so violent her mind shatters. Knowledge of the impossible. She wails a gut-wrenching sound.

The blackness, the thing without true shape will tear her apart and spit her out, her soul, her essence will be no more. She will be devoured and cease to exist.

Exit all light, all thoughts.

The ultimate destruction is coming. The final end.

The payment of her is received and accepted.

A door bursts into life around her new enemies. A shaft of light, a tunnel, an entrance to a new place.

They leave without looking back, four in a line, led by Alex. There is no pity, no grief, no apologies, no explanation, only deep indifference, the coldest of all goodbyes. Anna will be forgotten. Erased. No one will miss her, no one will care.

She was surrounded by people and still completely alone.

"Please, no, please," she begs. Who can hear her, who can help?

This isn't happening, this can't be.

Discarded again, thrown away without a care.

The unyielding darkness lands on her, she feels the pressure of its hit first, the heaviness, the intolerable misery swallowing her. She thought she knew agony; thought she understood pain. She believed both were old and familiar friends.

She discovers so much more.

***

Anna dreams of memories that are not her own.

Bethany, beautiful Bethany with her pretty hair and light. She was darkness too, after all, her fraudulent shine was little more than a convincing glitter lure to capture.

She saw Anna's pain and turmoil, saw her misery, and pounced with hunger.

Anna was not the first. The private place in the vegetable garden, the area she was never supposed to tread, is where bodies lay buried, rotting, and forgotten. Skeletons of four.

Two men and two women. A young man was enticed into the group like her, he was someone's son, brother, or father. Two women, invited into Kingdom House and promised glory, someone's mother, daughters, or sisters. Alex wielded the knife that ended all of their lives. His father lies there too. Not dead in a car accident but killed by the poison his son gave him in a drink laced with the cold intentions of patricide.

Him, Alex, with his chiseled face and mystery, his cruelty and callousness.

A vile plot unfolded; one she had no understanding of. Acts of evil and malicious whispers. Her paranoia was the truth.

Her instinct warned her, and she failed to hear, refusing to listen to every doubt.

Barbaric-designed rituals all called for an offering. A person with a natural gift, willingly stepping into alternate worlds by spiritual means for the purpose of destruction, food for something other.

Her. Anna. A meal of energy and nothing more, just like the ones who came before her.

As she suffocates, wrapped in blacker than black hurt, she yearns to give in.

Life and now death truly is pain.

Her mind understands that fighting is useless. She is trapped, caught in an enemy embrace that is crushing her slowly.

Brutality, she has never known a life without suffering. Hope is dead.

What was she but a thing to use and discard? She was never seen for who she is, never heard. Promises spoken to her were forever broken.

Where was the empathy in life, the compassion, the pity?

Violence, for her, became ordinary. Solitude was expected and agony was entirely normal. She never belonged at all. She was a target, a person to manipulate. A toy, a game, a puppet.

She sliced her skin before she joined the fated group. Deep cuts to punish or remind.

No one loved her.
No one cared for her.
No one wanted her.
Alex used her.

Trickster ways and fake smiles, that's all life cared to show her. There will be no redemption now, and no salvation.

Existence is pitiful. Life dealt her a wicked blow and now it truly will end.

Falling, falling, down and down.

She hears madness approach and can feel it biting away at her soul with rotten, rancid fangs.

Whisper sounds assault her. Wretched words spoken by vile unseen tongues of infecting hate and a million lies. Every cruel word ever once spoken gave birth to the damned and fluttering beings descending upon her.

She will shatter.

Anna became blinded. Her eyes were wide open and shut simultaneously. Her own sight was pointless when she failed to see the truth. There is beauty in lies that are spoken so softly, so tenderly.

Her faith was placed in deceitful hands that only sought to harm.

She believed, believed she was wanted and now she plummets down. Yet there were stars in perfect lines, she saw genuine beauty.

She could fly once, and the sky was made of amethyst.

There was a bookstore, where it all began. She had a bedsit and a job she despised.

There were two options to take, and the wrong path was chosen.

Spikes of grief pierce her soul; Anna can only scream in vibrant agony.

Every last drop of hope she possesses leaks out of her, every desire and aim for the future.

Didn't she once have aspirations and dreams of her own?

She wanted a home, a husband and children. Ordinary things even the cruel succeed in having.

Hopelessness. Any good memories she had are being ripped away, any pleasant thought she once had is vanishing.

She cannot hold her mind together, she can feel a break, a separation. Her thoughts collide and shatter. Consciousness explodes. She hangs in space and time, ripping, tearing. Atom after atom.

Fresh waves of agony begin to pull her apart. All she can do is howl and cry.

She is fleshless, but skin rips from muscle and nerve. Bones she doesn't possess break and snap, sinew is chewed and mauled.

Unimaginable pain snaps her in two. She falls but does not move.

End it, end it all. Please.

She wants her enemy mind to quiet, for life to cease.

Thinking is painful. Memories are poison and pain comes anew. There must be peace in silence. Becoming nothing can be the ultimate quiet bliss.

How cruel life was. The injustice, the unfairness and now she faces death so complete she cannot fathom such an ending.

I should have known; I should have realised.

Her suspicions were not from past hurt but born from instinct and wisdom, from experience. Patterns only ever know how to repeat.

What will become of her memories, will a part of her still be aware and suffering?

Why must the guilty always win?

The rage she possesses as her own sparks into graphic life. Anger is the fuel that drives her inner strength.

The face of Alex fills her mind. What a fool she was to have things so badly wrong.

She finds she wants to track him down and kill him slowly, with delicious intent. He should be torn apart, not her and so should the others. A storm of regrets, why didn't she let her rage loose when she lived? Fury is clarity.

Bites begin, small and savage, vicious, snapping bites. Each new attack brings heightened levels of fresh pain.

She has to fight but where is her strength? Gone.

Revenge.

Those familiar syllables.

The word sparks and sends a shimmer of fire throughout her essence.

Now it is her who speaks with feelings.

There is no greater wrath than a woman scorned, a woman mutilated by life and tarnished by hate. It is a thing to fear, a feat of shock and awe far beyond the boundaries of normality.

Pain is clarity.

She is beaten and yet she should do nothing but accept.

No.

She refuses.

Fight.

Agony and misery both love company.

Innocence lost. She plummets down, dropping from one world and entering the next.

Fight, fight, fight.

She embraces the wild scorching tearing through her. She was becoming whole and now the careful threads are undone.

No.

NO.

ENOUGH.

She roars in waves of emotion.

She will not end her awareness without correction.

Pain is not her enemy. Pain is her friend, pain is clarity. She knows it all too well and can use it.

133

Power engulfs her, heat and vile stinging sensations.

Swallowed whole she falls deeper until a loud silence fills her. She drifts into oblivion. Frozen or paused, a temporary respite.

Time passes and means nothing.

She is darker than her surroundings. She has no sight, no senses left, only tangled thoughts too heavy to properly unwind.

There is hardly anything left of her, only strips and rags with raw edges.

A vast shape emerges, and creeps nearer, she can feel its approach, its sudden awareness, and keen interest.

It knows her, from past and future times. From before and after.

It is vividly alive, a thinking entity, a thing that slithers and crawls within dark places only. A hive mind of brutal deeds, a collective of wicked torment and corruption in the guise of formidable beauty. Anna feels her vision return and fill with bright rainbow shades.

Reds and purples, greens and shades of yellow. She had forgotten glorious sights could exist.

The being, the entity, the mind, is made of sharp and spiteful glass shards arranged into a chaotic, jagged pattern of immense size. A prism, a sacred geometrical design of huge proportions. It shimmers and quivers, rippling with power and force. Liquid, plasma, gas and solid.

Everything and nothing, death and life, chaos and calmness. Infinite.

Each piece, every shard of it catches the bright shine of a light that doesn't exist. A prism entity with licks of flames running wild inside. A swirling tornado of vile ideas. It is all knowledge, a mind, all pulse, and mystery. She is tiny against it. The jagged shape moves and forms into a smooth glass-like sphere, with patterns flickering inside.

Anna hangs in judgement, captured, caught by incomprehension.

An invasion occurs. She feels an invisible presence inside what remains of her, poking and biting at her torn and ruined soul, exploring.

It scans and reads her fractured thoughts and memories, feeling her hate and desire for destruction.

It speaks inside her mind, whispers gently. Its voice feels like warm silk dripping with fresh honey. It knew her fate, it bellowed loudly but she failed to hear, refused to listen.

Friend or foe. Friend. Ally. Feminine rage. The pain of those innocent fallen in times gone before and after, a collective.

The energy of fear and violence swarmed together and formed shape.

It can use her. She has darkness inside, rot, a rawness, and an open and festering wound.

Opportunity beckons. She has been seen. The thing made of prisms and fire wraps tightly around her. It wants her, it needs her.

Shards of pure torture burst inside. The agony is a delight of hurt to endure.

A split, a tear, a shred. Pain and pleasure beyond ideas. Two become one.

A deal is made. An exchange is brokered without negotiation.

Anna is to become different. Remade in the image of her hate, molded by the desire for revenge.

Deep changes occur.

The twisted emotions of rage, brutality, and violence recognize their reflection in her. Fury works to fashion something new. Vengeance is the fabric, the power.

Pain is purity.

Sparks fly and flames catch. Heat engulfs.

Anna once wished to be a phoenix and now she truly does burn.

***

Lost, as always. Anna wanders a land unknown to her. She is light no longer.

Her thoughts feel muddled and underwater. She cannot recall who she is, or what she is.

She stumbles, afraid.

Where is she and what happened?

It is too hard to think. Too difficult to understand. Nothing feels in order, in sync.

She sees a crooked group of trees, bare, with sharp branches and complex gnarled twists.

She does not feel whole, not complete. Rationality is absent, and all complex thought has fled.

A sound disturbs her, an odd noise. A clockwork dog moves in a haphazard fashion in front of her. It yaps loudly. She can see a key, wedged in its back, turning slowly.

She thinks nothing of it, this strange sight, although it is oddly familiar. Her half mind is busy, filled with images of white bones, and ripping tender flesh.

A sound echoes above her, crackling wood and creaking limbs. A huge spider crawls in slow and wicked stealthy movements. It creeps across the tree branches, leaving a rope-like web in its wake.

It pays her no mind. Anna only watches it go. The flash of deep red across its abdomen reminds her of the shape of a skull, a blood-dripping skull.

Blood.

137

Memories stir and wake, a small spark begins to catch.

Inside her is a burning desire for vengeance, retaliation, retribution, and revenge. She can feel the turmoil begin to simmer and boil.

In the distance, she sees a group of figures walking across a jagged hill, they each look like paper people, strung together and cut out of paper with sharp scissors and careful hands. Lost souls.

She does nothing, she has no interest in the peculiar sight, no curiosity.

A blank slate.

The sound of tinkling bells alerts her. Something is approaching, rolling like a manic tornado. The closer the figure comes, the more she sees. It's a neon bright human shape, covered in tiny silver jingling bells. The thing has bent itself into a hoop shape, hands gripping feet, a wheel rolling towards her at speed.

It grinds to a halt in front of her and sends a spiral of dust into the air. It is dressed as an old-fashioned bright court jester, from an era long ago forgotten, when Kings played at jousting and Queens enjoyed the view from a throne.

The starkness of it hurts her vision.

Anna stares, she is not afraid or worried. She is simply numb and devoid of thought.

"What are you?" It asks her.

Its face is melted flesh, covered in thick make-up that only makes it appear more horrific. One ear is missing, and one eye is little more than an empty socket filled with writhing pale maggots. A single one falls to the ground and wriggles away with haste.

Its painted-on smile does not match the wickedness of its intent, its sinister nature.

Anna remains silent. She does not know what she is, how can she answer such a question?

"What are you?" It repeats, louder. Its voice sounds like rough sandpaper. It reaches out a foot and pokes her with the pointy tip of its obscene red shoe. There is a yellow pom-pom on the end containing a solitary beady blue eye that blinks once.

She hates the jester and finds it repulsive.

In reply to its question, Anna screams with pure anger, a soundwave explodes from her form.

The jester staggers back in fits of giggles, bells jingling, and returns to the shape of a hoop.

It swerves away, a manic wheel, and disappears as quickly as it arrived.

Anna shuffles back and hides in the circle of dead trees. She stares at the rotten and rough bark and tries to recall what she is and how she came to be in such a strange place.

The world around her is alien, unnatural, and also curiously familiar.

Her legs, she brings them to her chest and sees criss-crossed lines of deep scarring underneath crisp burnt flesh. As she stares, the scars flash with amber-colored fire.

It means something, she knows that, but what?

Where am I? Her first fully coherent thought.

Have I died? What am I?

Memories are fragile, hers have become infested with disease.

Is this her afterlife? Forever trapped in a place with no real-time, alone and afraid.

Even in madness, she would still be sentient, still be aware.

Abandoned.

One word to sum up her entire life.

She wonders if she could be a raindrop, a single drop of water falling from the sky onto the soft feathers of a bird in flight across a vast ocean.

Or perhaps she could be born once more, into a kinder world that might embrace her, with a mother that has the right to claim the smooth-sounding, elegant name.

Consciousness. Energy. Vibrations. Universes. Frequency.

Is she an empty shell, discarded and thrown away? Will anyone miss her?

Was she ever loved and needed, was there anyone?

Alex. Kingdom House.

The words make her jolt in shock. Quick memories flash and collide. Forces beyond comprehension awaken inside.

No, no, no.

She screams a primal wail of violence. She remembers, she recalls.

Betrayal.

Overhead, a majestic white owl circles her. It swoops down and explodes in a shower of black fluttering butterfly-like creatures.

Her whispers. Her companions.

Each one scurries close and surrounds her, voices like unseen bats collecting in a murmur.

They spiral around her and lend her strength. She is not alone.

Anna, in her half-life, begins to understand. She isn't trapped. She can move, there is a door for her. There is an exit, a way to find those who are damned and unaware of their fate. She has a purpose.

Yes, the universe witnessed the constant trespassers, and what it saw it hated.

As the thoughts occur, the spiteful whispers reach a crescendo of piercing murmuring sounds.

She must move.

There is a shaft of light, one sliver of an open door just for her. She stands. She is singular in her goal. But there is a new obstacle arriving.

The ground ripples and quivers, two huge shapes grow and emerge, bursting into existence. Human-shaped, but crooked and large, imposing, and powerful.

She steps back in assessment.

They are obscenities. Monstrous entities with the scent of Sulphur. Beings forming with fresh abhorrent life, dream entities from someone's nightmares, made real inside The Void.

Bones pop and creak, and cartilage snaps.

Filthy tarnished yellow skeletons wrapped in brown rags stand before her. Both have several internal organs on show. Malignant inside-out entities. The tallest has a red pulsing liver hanging by purple veins from its rib cage. Blood trickles slowly. A beating heart, with arteries and throbbing valves, and tendrils, hangs from the other. It beats, and ticks like a clock.

Both move their jaws quickly, grinding rancid teeth until a manic chattering noise sounds. Anna understands the vile things will not let her pass, but they must.

She has been manipulated, threatened, bullied, and abused for her entire life. There was no relationship of any kind that wasn't toxic waste at its very core. She spent her entire existence afraid and alone.

Her old world didn't want her, human beings with all their arrogant ways only sought to harm her.

She will not allow such reckoning to happen in death too. Her desire and need for revenge overcome all sense of fear. She will not be stopped. Prevention is too late.

Surrounded by her whispers, she roars.

The tone she makes is pure hate, menace, and violence all contained within one complex sound.

The inside-out beings stumble back, and the brown rags fall to reveal their entire beings.

Old, pitted bones and rotten, ruined marrow. Senseless entities, animations without real meaning. She kicks one. A thigh bone comes loose and hits the ground. It is immediately swallowed, stolen, and devoured by the unnatural earth.

There is not a force able to stop her, except pure light or goodness and there is neither present.

She pounces, rips and shreds.

The skeletons explode. Bones fly through the air and land with loud rattles in multiple piles. The heart.

The beating heart one possesses is something she no longer has as her own. It lands by her feet and throbs, alive still. Before the jumbles of bones can reassemble, she picks it up and squeezes the wet warmth, feeling it tear and die under her given power. Blood, flesh, life, she hates it all.

She has been pulled apart and remade. The rage she held back, the fear she felt daily, the injustice, the worry, every negative aspect has been remodeled.

How easy it is to destroy; how good it feels. How natural and delicious. She licks her hand and exits, out through the door to elsewhere.

Her whispers follow eagerly. She does not look back.

***

Anna is inside the house she once called home. It seems like several lifetimes ago, an eternity. In truth, she understands that only a collection of minutes has passed since her death.

The scenes around her are grey. Devoid, emptied of all life.

Inside the room she died in, she sees her deceased body. She lays still, crooked like a broken doll, a pool of darkness spread around her.

The painted symbol on her forehead does not match the others. There was no owl of wisdom for her, she was simply marked with an X.

Blood. Life. Emptied. Gone. Her carcass will be wrapped in old blankets and buried in the vegetable garden, she will become compost, nourishing food for worms and nature. Recycled. She feels nothing but pity for what she once was. One single human life experience is nothing compared to what does exist. But it wasn't his to take. Alex, the sinner, and murderer.

The others are still alive, the grimmest reaper of all came only for her.

She can sense their thudding hearts, the wild rush of blood pounding through systems of intricate veins and arteries. Acts her own fallen body will never achieve again.

They each lie still, living but vacant, off exploring, at the cost of her life, her soul.

Yet they do not know all they think they know; opinions are not facts and theories are not proof.

The curse of humanity in one sentence. Ignorance is as prolific as a plague. Human beings are a parasitical race leaving nothing but carnage behind.

145

Anna steps forward and stares at each person.

Isabelle, with her motherly ways and her gentleness in tending her pointless wounds. All lies.

Bethany, her grace and sunshine. All fake, fraudulent light powered by deceit.

Matt, his quietness and thirst for knowledge. Arrogant traitor, guilty of inaction, its own kind of special evil.

Alex. The ringleader, narcissist, betrayer. Killer. Murderer. The worst one of all.

She hates each person. The emotion tastes bitter and sweet, rotten sugar, and sour honey covered in stings.

A wave of rage explodes around her, but no person is touched. They each sleep soundly, unbothered by her, souls busy exploring realms of glory without her.

How much she longs to rip each person to shreds. Here, in the physical world, she does not belong.

She lashes out at Alex; her see-through form fails to connect. She is a shimmer, he is solid. Frequency, and vibration, are all different and without matching.

Anna wails in frustration and howls with defeat. Now is the wrong time. It will come.

She retreats and waits.

146

*S*he bled her way into new worlds and now she steps with borrowed grace.

Anna has no idea how much time has passed but as she retreated, her half mind became lost and fled elsewhere.

Now, her senses are firing once more. Her rage is growing. Her fury is sacred.

There have been changes in her absence.

The room she stands in is her place of death, the floor is the site of her betrayal, sacrifice, and murder.

Wicked intentions and spiteful deeds, all hidden away from eyes that might see cold truths.

A Persian rug now covers her death spot, a fresh stain that used to be her. In the physical world, it is the only mark she left behind and all traces have been disguised and erased.

The thing, the shards of prism and flame she is now part of, now belongs to, is displeased by the scenes.

Invaders, trespassers, infiltrators.

She can feel the colours, the depths of anger spread inside until it becomes hard to know which emotion belongs to whom, perhaps there is no real difference.

Yet there are voices. Not her biting, curious whisper companions, but real human voices with their complex webs of words whose meanings she has forgotten. She follows the sound eagerly.

Her surroundings are half-familiar, intricate memories still stored in some cloud-like akashic hall of universal records, of data she has access to.

People. She knows them and recognizes each one in her mirror darkly. A quick jolt of fire-laden hate loosens the knowledge.

Enemies. Opponent. Foe. Nemesis absolutes. Vile cunts. A killer and consorts. Complicit all.

The words make her sour. She vibrates with turmoil and violence so dark it might swallow her.

Balance, she wanted such a thing, and yet it was always out of her reach.

Traitors. Betrayers.

There they stand, in the shiny surfaced kitchen, drinks in hand, smiling and laughing together. All four. The cacophony of happiness creates an abyss inside dark places.

The four cannot see her, they cannot sense her. For all of their walking in other worlds, they cannot feel another realm is pressing close.

Their life energy makes her sick, their heartbeat, their vibrancy, their current state of being.

She wants to end them all and destroy.

She understands that is why she still exists, why she still *is*.

The four have been marked as trespassers, unwelcome intruders into other realms. Their presence will not be tolerated further. The natural order is in confusion, and it is their fault. Transition is transgression. Dimensions should not be hacked, not be shortcut by spell craft and ritual, by cheating and trickery, and wild sorcery.

Hidden ways and secrets, the forbidden information they hold cannot be allowed to spread. Unwelcome invaders in places where none should be.

The knowledge is secret for reasons.

Only life and death, and the true source of all control the infinite, controls transmissions and the alteration of states.

She screams a high-pitched shriek, aiming for a show of force. A shock and awe attack. Nothing happens. No one can hear her furious wrath.

She steps closer, reaches out, and touches Bethany's soft hair. The woman only frowns and shakes her head, running a hand through her hair in confusion.

"Kill…you," Anna whispers.

There is no structure to her words, she sounds like the wild hissing of a snake or radio static lost within the depths of space.

No one can hear her.

The four enemies have no idea how near she stands, how close her new world is pushing against their own.

"Can anyone smell smoke?" Isabelle asks.

"Probably the candles," the smooth-tongued liar Alex answers. "I blew them out."

"I'll check."

Isabelle comes quickly towards her. Before she can move, the older woman walks straight through her form. Anna feels the brief invasion and staggers, repulsed by the sudden flash of humming life and energy.

The woman stops and tilts her head, sensing strangeness, unsure.

"Are you okay Mother," Matt asks.

Mother?

She hates the pretty word, two syllables that for her, mean neglect and abandonment.

150

Yet the name is wrong, it isn't appropriate, is it?

"Yes, I'm fine," the older woman answers.

Mother, mother, mother.

The word begins to echo and rebound. The scene becomes vaguely jagged and out of sync.

When she returns to herself, her group of nemesis is still together, laughing and clinking glasses. A celebration is occurring. The energy of joy fills the room and pushes her away. Happiness is still untouchable.

Now what?

She retreats once more and wanders the house that used to be home. It was death row for her, and she never knew a countdown had been placed upon her head. The executioner came to collect, and he did so with sheer cruelty.

She finds herself in the room that used to be hers. Nothing of her old self remains, not even a scent.

Existence wiped clean away.

What use was sending her to stop trespassers without her being able to touch a thing?

Cause and effect. Chaos theory. Pain is purity. Wait, what is that?

Mirror, mirror on the wall, who's the fairest of them all?

Anna is.

She can see herself; she views her appearance. She is not made of translucent light any longer.

She has a temporary structure. A foot in several worlds.

Her flesh, or some perversion of it, is blackened and charred, burned beyond all recognition. Puffs of smoke rise, as if she just stepped out of some wild bonfire. Lightning streaks of glowing amber flames sit in place of her heavy scars. Her eyes are the brightest of blue and deep, primordial darkness. Sharp fins line her arms and chest, jagged and razor sharp. She appears androgynous, gender has been stripped away, although she feels feminine. Wronged in a way only a woman can understand. Anna raises her chin and turns her head, admiring her reflection. The sharp arch of her cheekbone is edged and smooth, the bare skull she possesses is dark and embedded with thorns like a pretty rose made of vicious and nasty parts.

Her hands are strong and graced with fierce talons in place of nails.

Beauty, glory, she sees both and has become what she craved to witness. She hisses loudly, her cracked lips part revealing rows of rotten fangs for teeth.

Familiarity rises. She knows.

Revenge.

It was her. Did she warn her former self of her fate to no avail? How?

Time repeats, a loop that cannot be broken. Linear time shattered, straight became twisted into circular. All possibilities exist. The fabric of time and space has been ripped and torn.

A contradictory universe of pleasure and anguish.

False structures, clocks ticking. The fourth dimension can come undone and rewind, play again.

The concept feels meaningless. Why would she attempt to stop fate or try to give herself a clue? Why would she want to prevent herself from being reborn into a vision of absolute glory?

She rejects the path of destiny.

Anna is as she was fashioned to be. Revenge constructed lethality. Yet how is she supposed to hurt those who hurt her?

Frantic whispers swarm her, dark shadows of biting chaos. Instructions are given and spoken with caution.

She is all power, not cracked apart. Special gifts were given, skills for the already talented. She was chosen and picked, selected for greatness.

She has been reborn as something else, something old, ancient, and yet brand new. Misery attracts misery, an agreement was made.

The assassinated has become a fractured assassin.

She moves and steps gracefully across the plush carpet she cannot truly feel.

There is a way to unleash her fury. There is always a way. She only had to wait to be guided.

The room at the end of the hall is where Alex sleeps without regrets or nightmares plaguing him.

The speaker of all lies. The sex between them was a distraction, a way for him to lure her to trust him. He knew her doubt, her worry, and compelled her with a meaningless promise. A trick. Advantage taken. A chess match, it was the moment she lost a game she was not aware she was playing.

Anna watches him without compassion. She feels no love, no remorse. She can only wait with cold calculation. Patience is a virtue, and it is her only one.

Every human being is rich with faults and flaws. Sin, greed, and the endless need to feed the ego exist inside most. Light and darkness, an epic battle.

She wasn't full of holes and weakness. She was only guilty of clinging to hope, and it became her death sentence.

Trust was a rope with which to hang her.

She did not expect to find true meaning, true life, inside the layers of annihilation.

She wanders away, drifts as if she is nothing, and finds herself outside.

She can feel the humming power of dead bones, a vibration inside that tells her where murdered bodies lie forever sleeping, including her own.

New energy too, growing things to eat and enjoy, fed by the decay of rotting human beings.

She ignores the lure and moves, searching for weak spots, strings, and membranes to follow and pierce.

The first one she senses; she pushes in and through. Past, future, present, parallel, alternate, she understands true secrets.

Vibration, frequency, tuning in a radio dial. She can pick and choose any station, any world. Pierce the layers without disturbance.

There are places, realms no human should tread, but she can. Endless levels, the many mansions spoken of.

Inside her is the wild urge, the desire to see more glorious things.

The landscape she exits into has red sand. She finds the sight appealing but cannot say or comprehend why.

A vast ocean of liquid mercury faces her, smooth, molten metal churning in the middle. A massive creature emerges, a leviathan of a beast. Thick scales cover its entire body, while eyes of bright amber assess its surroundings. It roars with glory; she feels the shaking inside.

It truly is magnificent, primal, a hungry force awakening. A tidal wave of liquid mercury forms itself into a wave and heads towards her.

She does not move; all fear is removed. The heat cascades over her, burning brightly, boiling the force she inhabits, creating fierce armor on her shape and structure.

Violence, destruction, rebirth, she stands and embraces all. Pain so vibrant engulfs her, she finds the sensation to be a wicked delight.

Around her feet splash the smallest of creatures, hundreds of them, washed up in the ocean of turmoil.

She bends carefully and picks one up. Immediately it shrieks a high-pitched wail, adverse and disgusted by her touch.

The thing she holds is curious, a faceless cone-shaped body with lashing tentacles that sting.

It wants to bite and cause hurt, the only nature it will ever know.

She flings it far away, bored. In the distance, soft glowing lights appear. Souls lost or dreamers dreaming, their consciousness briefly slipping into strange places that won't be recalled.

She can terrorize and chase, tear and rip, shred to pieces, and yet she chooses not to.

Only the leviathan creature interests her, the way it rages with such anger and violence, contempt and intolerance. She understands it and recognizes that she too, is the same.

***

She finds herself in the place she once lived.
A day or three has gone by, Anna is not sure. The sun came up and then it was gone. The moon appeared and took its place several times.

She prefers the darkness. Layers of night hide slithering, nasty things and now it hides her too.

She waits in the room she died in and understands her time to strike will be soon. The guilty four are taking a substance to aid in astral projection. One world will never be enough.

Their bodies will be vacant, empty.

How many levels exist after life is over? How many tunnels of light or drops down are present? How many doors, grey worlds, or places where flowers grow in wild abundance? Endless.

How many were lost and how many, like her, have been found and salvaged?

157

Reality is stranger than any mind can comprehend. Level after level for eternity and restrictions, walls are in place.

Other realms were never their own to walk, never theirs to lay claim on. Rules were bypassed, loopholes found, and errors were noticed. A door swung open, and a lock was broken.

Visits to places angels fear to tread are not allowed. Infiltrators.

Revenge.

Time flickers and passes with haste. Tick tock.

She watches as the souls, the light of Bethany, Matt, and Isabelle lift and soars skywards like tiny rockets. None register her presence, eagerness, and greed can be blinding.

She watches Alex, her dark eyes burning with sexual passion stuck in reverse.

Up he rises. His light is brighter than ever. Out from the layers of darkness and shadow, she steps.

Frequencies are changed. Vibrations are altered. She sees his soul escape; he does not see her new nature.

Anna drops down, creeping slowly, a slither.

He pushed his way into her body and now she will do the same to him.

Pain is purity and now she is the teacher, the slave is the master.

She suffers more now. Her essence, her soul has been ripped in two. Broken apart in a tidal wave of injustice.

She feels the rage that fuels her, the power, the desire to punish and win. She embraces all.

There is purity in pain, *emotional* pain, the fools had it wrong. Physical pain is an error. Inner hurt is the thing that transcends and causes change.

Damnation was always fated to be her gift.

Whispers swarm like birds around her, circling, aiding, advising.

'Slowly, carefully,' they place suggestions inside her mind.

She merges with the body of Alex, a half-life, possession of a temporary kind.

Her essence, wrapped in his body, feels violently alien and unnatural. Heavy and full of lead. Stifling and chaotic.

It feels absurd to breathe, as if she is drowning in air.

How awkward he feels, how rigid and conforming, heavy. Restrictive and full of pressure. The join riddles her mind with thick disorientation.

Thoughts assault her, memories he left behind.

Bethany as a child, all blonde hair and loveliness. Images of his father, a more arrogant man than him. Stern and unloving, focused, and single-minded.

A man who searched tirelessly for answers and found few. Alex encouraged and led to follow in his intimidating footsteps until he drank the poison that ended him.

The kills.

The murders of two young women, used just like her, and one man. The thrill he felt, the power and control. He enjoyed it all and relished the power.

She cares not for the fallen and only for herself. She is pain now. She is other.

She sits up in the body of Alex, a puppet master, without the need for pitiful strings for control.

Time is meaningless for her, yet she also understands she must rush.

With clumsy steps, she stumbles and jerks into the kitchen, falls, and hauls herself up. Her borrowed legs are heavy, clumsy, a suit of heavy iron.

She knows the house well enough, knows where the biggest and sharpest knives are.

It is difficult to grip a heavy object and yet easy to slice the throat of Isabelle. Blood pours easily, spilling like hot red milk.

160

Curious, she pulls the wound apart, peering at raw flesh and meaty gristle.

Acts, theatre, plays. Her four enemies wore convincing masks, guards were raised, and not once did they falter.

The matriarch.

Isabelle is the mother of Alex, Matt, and Bethany. As knowledge floods, a ripple of surprise jolts her. For three months they kept up such an act. Did they want to be seen as individuals joined together with one common goal in mind and not the sadistic family they truly are? Or was she meant to be reassured by the apparent newness of Matt?

Golden pretty lies.

Anna only wants their deaths and craves them. She doesn't care who they were in life anymore, it only matters that they die.

Matt is next and now her cruelty knows no bounds. She hates indifference, *hates it.*

He is the epitome of.

She cuts the flesh of his face, wishing he could feel every beautiful and bitter slice. Down the side, from temple to chin, she forces the blade to move. She can feel his heart beating. Thud, thud, thud.

Older brother.

So that's who he is. Tricks and lies with pitch black tar for a soul. He wasn't his father's favourite and wasn't his mother's best child either.

She grips tightly and yanks the thick skin of his face. She hears the rip, the delicious tear of flesh from nerve, sinew, and muscle. The sound is exciting to her, it is music.

How strange people look underneath their skin, how raw and similar. Anna, bored with her plaything, slices his throat in one deep swipe. As an afterthought, she pokes her borrowed thumb into his eye socket and enjoys the loud popping noise. Vitreous gel and blood pour, shiny and watery. She isn't impressed.

Beautiful Bethany is next, with her sweetness and lures.

How easily Anna was enthralled by her, how quickly she was lost.

The girl can sense weakness and now Anna has none.

She moves and crawls, freezes into place. There is a problem of some magnitude.

Bethany is awake, back in her body, and sitting up, alert, and bewildered.

Did the woman sense a disturbance within The Void?

Is Alex attempting to return and instead, found his body has been taken and possessed?

Human eyes are not equipped, not gifted enough to witness the full light spectrum. If Alex is present, she cannot see him with her borrowed human eyes.

162

"Alex," Bethany whispers. "What are you doing! What have you done?"

Her voice is croaky, hoarse. She is clearly disoriented and confused.

Anna, a mere passenger, acts quickly and scrambles towards her, crawling on her hands and knees. Twice, she slips in pools of blood. Bethany screams loudly and jumps to her bare feet.

Anna cannot allow her to escape, survival is not an option. The body she inhabits is too heavy, a clumsy metal suit of iron. She propels herself up, dives, and manages to grab a fist full of Bethany's soft hair.

The slender woman falls backward, hits the floor, and immediately begins kicking and punching.

Anna feels her borrowed nose explode, she feels the hurt and it is nothing. It only makes her more savage, and more determined.

She raises her muscular arm, forms an awkward fist, and punches. Bethany cries out once and falls still, her feet twitching madly. Anna straddles her and watches intently, deciding. It was a mistake to think she could kill them all without incident. But she has her now. Let Bethany choke, let her die without the essential air she needs. She wraps her huge hands around her delicate throat and squeezes with brutal force.

Bones break under the pressure, life drains away, and breathing is restricted.

Her body spasms, and buckles. Anna presses tighter, tighter until the heart of the girl ceases its frantic beating and stops.

There is only one place the essence of her will shift to, only one place that will snatch her soul.

Can the others feel their death occur in another realm? No, Anna felt nothing of her bodily pain. Only her cord fell away and shattered.

Let all three suffer, let all three experience the terror she felt. Let there be no remorse and certainly no mercy.

She stands and stumbles, trying to think with her own mind and not the echo of the brain she currently inhabits.

Alex.

She can feel a part of him left behind. A cold and callous man, skillful at deception. Arrogant. He only cares for himself and believes he is deserving of the greatest answers. Fake superiority. He yearns to exist in a higher realm, with a view of greatness. He wished to transcend.

She wants Alex to suffer the most, a quick death is too good for him. Two of the others are enclosed within the boundaries of The Void, the entity of prism and flame tells her so, one is on her way. As for Alex, he

164

deserves much more sweet and prolonged agony.

She lifts the receiver of the phone in the hallway and dials the emergency services with several awkward jabs of one finger. She will leave him alive. Let him have a lifetime to wallow and think, let her visit him in the confines of a cell and torment him, let her feed from his misery until she snatches his soul clean away.

How the mighty have fallen so easily, almost.

Dominoes cascading in a line.

"I killed them," she slurs and tells the person who answers. Her voice is male and smooth and for a moment, it surprises her. She laughs. Saliva drips down her temporary chin. "I'm Alex and I killed them all."

A confession.

There is no need to say anything more in the voice that is not her own. The call will be traced quickly enough, help and police will arrive.

What will they find? Murdered bodies, illegal substances, occult paraphernalia, ritual, and symbology. The killer will be found alive and unable to deny his guilt.

Whispers, her teasing friends of mass and oddness collect around her. Ideas of wickedness and cruelty are placed in her mind.

Anna smiles.

Yes, yes, she will. Why not?

She pulls down the plain and loose linen trousers of the body she has invaded.

How odd it feels to temporarily own a penis, how peculiar. It once gave her pleasure, only once, and now it looks ugly and shriveled. It must sense its fate, must know its future.

She takes the base and stretches, laughing gleefully.

She raises her arm and drops her knife as if she is holding a machete or cleaver. The first impact slices through spongy tissue and skin. One shredded nerve hangs out and wiggles like a caught and frantic garden worm.

She feels the exquisite roar of pain and a manic kind of happiness.

Punish. Punish. Punish.

One more heavy blow and off it comes, a blob of unrecognizable mush in her hand.

She shrieks in triumph and throws it against the clean white wall. The goo slides down and leaves a slimy blood trail in its wake.

What a surprise Alex will have when he returns alone, what terror he will feel, what hell on earth he will face.

Will his pain still be purity? Anna laughs.

She stumbles and crawls her way back into the room with the dead bodies, the ritual room. One more task, she must destroy the book, burn it as she burned.

The vessel she occupies is leaking blood and weakening. She scrambles to the book of Hidden Fragments and sets a candle flame against it. Fire. From birth the force is ravenous, and hungers without end. Given the chance, greedy flames would devour the world and still demand more.

Pages catch, ancient secrets, instructions and forbidden knowledge become parchments of smoke and ash. Page after page is quickly destroyed. The instruction manual for the damned is no more.

As sirens begin to sound, closer, nearer, she leaves the puppet she animates. The body of Alex crumples to the floor, awaiting his return.

***

Seven unholy paths, seven deadly sins, pride, greed, lust, envy, gluttony, wrath, and sloth.

Deadly yes, but together, delicious Deliverance.

Anna moves through the world with a singular purpose. Down the twisting path and out into the night.

Bright red and blue lights explode in the sky and ruin the shades of darkness she prefers. Still, she welcomes the sight, justice inside their steel horses have arrived.

Three have fallen. One, if he survives, will suffer prolonged punishment and when he truly dies, she will hunt his soul down like a bloodhound. There will be no escape for Alex, no mercy shown.

Yet her enemy list is a long one. Why should she stop? How many times did she complain there was no balance in the world, how many have hurt her and tarnished her with stains that could never have been removed?

She *is* balance now.

She is the weigher of sins and her enemies have been found lacking. How can she achieve fulfilment when such evil exists in her old world?

Suffering, agony, pain, she knew it all. The turmoil of being used, of broken trust, of wicked abuse.

All she saw was hypocrisy and hate and now she has become both of those things.

Whispers surround her and offer her redemption, a chance to become whole. The being of prisms and flame seeks her return and calls for her to join it.

She refuses, for now.

Her biting whispers aid her in choosing one special door back to The Void, the place with the doorways. She wants to see, needs to witness.

There is no moving through time and space, she simply steps and finds herself in the realm that was so frightening. She is made, cut from the same fabric of this reality. She understands what it all means, what it all is, and the hidden knowledge she craved and thought valuable now feels irrelevant.

She can see it all laid out as a web inside her mind.

Cold truths.

There were never any higher realms to aim for and explore. Upper levels were mere phantoms, out of reach mirages, lies, and not for them.

The doorways higher, those bathed with white-ended tunnels, exist only for the kind, for those whose good deeds outweigh the bad upon death.

Judgement does exist.

There is no access for those with still living bodies, no cheat code. Every out-of-body soul travel carried out with instructions from the wretched book had only one singular direction. Down. Lower. Below, under, back to the place she knew from before.

Conversations with divinity, with higher beings, are carried out by enemies with deceitful natures, and illusions of grandeur. Masked entities with liquid lies.

Those four arrogant fools failed to see the truth of reality.

Anna does not care; she is part of something else now.

Whatever she was before is meaningless, she only holds the power of fury and hate.

Quickly, she searches and senses with her half mind. Tendrils of black spirals spring from her body and act as scouts, alert, and hunting.

She knows. She can feel where they are. The three, the fourth remains alive, rescued from death temporarily.

She moves with stealth, past the church set in reverse with its faceless congregation.

It *is* a house of worship, and those souls inside issue a constant plea for help. The begging of a few who still believe an almighty force might swoop down and rescue them with a careful hand and white feathered wings.

An ultimate force, a great old one does exist in this place, but it isn't made of love or goodness but the opposite.

All possibilities exist, including a realm, a layer without light or love present. A place where hope is not welcome. Energy does not die and can never be destroyed. Depravity collected, evil deeds over countless centuries came together and The Void was born and created. A realm of crooked reverse.

Nightmares burst into existence; all manner of creatures created by multiple minds.

Life is but a dream.

She arrives at the chasm she once viewed with fear and gazes at the screaming faces suffering in the wild flames. Isabelle and Matt. Mother and son. Both are almost unrecognizable, trapped for eternity in sheer agony, part of the endless fire that consumes. Caught and captured. Burning forever, without redemption or salvation. Souls lost.

Anna is pleased by the magnificent sight.

But where is the third?

Bethany, she finds her screaming, hanging upside down from a dead tree, bound by sharp barbed wire wrapped around one leg. Bird-like creatures made of black feathers, lies, and perversion peck at her without remorse. One uses its fierce beak to open her side, a blood dripping organ is swiftly pulled free and fought over.

Old Greek myth, Prometheus in chains, fashioned into a new, more modern form.

Each bite can be felt. Each morsel, each chunk of flesh taken grows back quickly and is soon feasted on again. Anna sits, watches the artful display, and listens to the wretched wails that have become her preferred source of pleasure.

She places a hand on the ground and feels it stir. Her ruthless acts make the land stronger, firmer, and more bitter, but she can aid fate.

171

As Bethany screams in terror, in violent madness, she sees her. Her eyes grow wide in acknowledgment. Consciousness sees consciousness, or some version of, and recognizes.

Bethany began the chain of consequences that caused her personal downfall. The rolling ball was first kicked by her.

Now it is she who pleads for help, for assistance. Now it is her who receives none.

Anna listens to the beautiful sounds of agony until time passes. She grows bored and leaves.

There is a spark of life to observe.

Her biting whispers guide the way.

The four or maybe those who came before them opened a new Pandora's box. Peeling back layers causes vulnerabilities in the fabric of universes.

Weak spots. Holes. Corruption and darkness are leaking into her old world. Wickedness is seeking comfort in spiteful deeds. Masks are worn and fear will be eaten, devoured as a meal.

The manipulation of humanity draws near.

Why should forgiveness exist? People know what the fuck it is they are doing.

Sleeping giants stir with wild anticipation, beings of unfathomable size seek nourishment, change, and destruction.
The single doorway to exit, the tear in the veil, she leaves it wide open with sheer purpose, cruel intentions. A trickle is not enough, let there be a flood, a revelation.

The realm of The Void is let free, set loose. Anna is as she was made to be.

*A*lex.

Handcuffed. Chained and drugged with painkillers, an officer of the law on guard outside. The killer is lying in a hospital bed in a building designed to heal. How weak he appears, how drained and empty.

A grey man, with all colour missing.

His family is gone, torn away from him just like his ruined penis. His only future is behind the bars of a cell.

His special book is burned and charred, just as she is. The forbidden magic turned to ash and died.

Cause and effect in action.

Anna feels powerful, full of pulsing vibrating energy. Alex cannot see her, but he can feel her and sense her nearness as she grows stronger. She can see his body tense; the scent of fear fills the air.

174

Any feelings she had for him have vanished and love? She cannot recall the emotion or remember the meaning.

Whispers assist and lend her a voice.

"Your family is suffering for eternity," she hisses. "Mother burns in a pretty fire."

She feels his heart quicken and start to beat rapidly. His entire body begins to shake and jerk. A single tear rolls down his cheek.

"No, no, no," he repeats in disbelief.

Oh yes.

Panic, fear, wonderful emotions to absorb and embrace.

Now he will be her plaything, he will be her game. She will visit him often and cause his mind to decay, she will watch his undoing and stare as the rot spreads.

"Doors work two ways," she reminds him. "This place will burn."

He knew nothing. A fake teacher, a fraud, a liar, a fool.

Now he jolts in turmoil, loud alarms sound and so she leaves. There will be plenty of time to torture. The end will be a slow death for most, a prolonged act.

Anna wants to walk in the world that used to be hers. The world that failed to help her, or offer her any warmth, compassion or protection. The realm of dishonesty and vileness, the place that needs to plummet.

Multiple exits open.

She does not take them, yet, and maybe not at all.

Why shouldn't she be vengeance, a voice for those who lack their own?

Every house she passes contains secrets, in every person and family. Some are dark and bitter, twisted. Why shouldn't she destroy those who aim to feed their own perversions at the cost of others?

Human beings, she wants to devour, absorb until she becomes satiated or something close to.

She will punish and frighten, terrorize and threaten. All victims need a voice. She is still unseen but now this works in her favour.

She is needed, wanted. She will become balance in a world that has none, a weigher of sins.

She yearned to see true beauty and now it surrounds her.

There are rippling shadows, shades, and souls of the dead leaking in from below, creeping in from The Void. Human eyes, living witnesses cannot see, yet, but she can see all.

Human beings have one new fate, most are destined to be the playthings of an older, ancient, powerful collection of entities. Cosmic annihilators. Eaters of sin and disgrace.

Trickster beings. Forces of life that existed before cell division, before planets

176

exploded and crashed together, before the sun was born, and before light was ever a concept.

Before the beginning.

Entities with a thousand faces, a thousand masks, and a million intricate fraudulent ways. They wait with borrowed skins and bloody costumes.

She can see it all laid out as a web inside her mind.

New slithering forms are seeping in through tiny slivers and cracks. All go off to search and hunt, relentless with hunger. Parasites with one desire to infect and cause ruination. Entities with a hundred different names given to them over the centuries. Each one is starved.

She watches as a human woman walks alone, heels click-clacking on the pavement. A thing walks with her, hovering close, a nameless dark entity, all light is absent. It follows and stalks, causing the stranger deep unease without a true source, creating her misery, her fear, and eating the emotions, the turmoil.

Anna is not the only thing that likes to cause pain and destruction. Both are her purpose and there are thousands just like her.

The streets are starting to fill, two worlds are beginning to collide.

The pavement ripples, like heat on the tarmac. A thing rises, all jagged and crooked in shape. Angular sharp limbs and darkness. It stretches wildly, joints popping and snapping. A huge ink spot with thick creeping legs.

Neighborhood dogs begin to bark, sensing the invasion. Cats out prowling, hiss, and run away.

The fabric of the sky is splitting at the seams and no human alive understands what is next. Something wicked this way comes and with it, is suffering and fire.

A multitude of cries erupts from the lost, the broken, the silent screamers, the ones who cannot rest without revenge, the killed unfairly, things with hate for flesh, and chaos for bone.

The Void is merging with her old world. An army is arriving, a legion with brutal intentions. An invasion, a soon to be occurring massacre.

The jester she met appears, and races along the street as a hoop, its bells jingling wildly, off to cause wonderful havoc and fatal pranks.

"I see you!" It yells at her.

Darkness can sense its own, evil can recognize its reflection, and wickedness will search not for the righteous, not for the kind, but for the immoral, the corrupt among society. Those without love in their hearts. There are more than enough to feast upon. A banquet.

There, the tall man walking alone, leaving the limited safety of his home.

She can feel the pulse of wretchedness inside him. He is a signal, a beacon shining with terrible past and present deeds.

An angry man, callous and cruel, who uses fists and violence as a control method. Entities swarm him, and form a circle around him, swooping and diving down. He can sense the nearness of terror, and how closely it bites at him. He quickens his step, his fear rising, unable to see what plagues him.

He will be pulled apart in judgement soon enough, torn to shreds and eaten with greed, tortured until only madness becomes his sole chance of escape.

Delicious.

And her, the well-dressed woman exiting her expensive car. How corrupt she is, with her backhanded deals and bribery. A woman in a position of power and her greed became too vast. Her ego overtook her ability to follow the law. See how she looks down upon society with narcissistic contempt. Look how she regards herself as better than all. As she walks, bleak impenetrable shapes surround her, they will be her undoing. She speeds up, her instinct is warning her an enemy lurks close. Too late, vile beings want her ruthlessness for themselves.

Her old world is becoming different.

It is or soon will be, absolute Hell on Earth.

Accompanied by her damned whispering biting companions, Anna walks. This time, her head is held high.

She is charred, she is burned, decorated with sharp razor fins, and she is beautiful.

She is the monster behind you on a cold dark night, the creeping shadow you catch in the corner of your eye, the creature you sense is lurking close, the mystery you cannot solve. The curse in your life, the vile thing hiding under your bed, the wickedness present around you.

The entity who whispers very bad things, the hostility encouraging sin, the being that stalks and destroys, rips you to shreds. It is her nature, and all hope is lost.

The prism of colour and flames was right to pull her apart and fate was right to choose her after all.

*This, a*s she is, was her destiny all along.

Her lifelong suffering meant something. It helped create what she has become. Foundations of hurt constructed anew.

The why or how is now irrelevant to her.

Let existence burn. Let the corrupt fall. Let her watch the firework display and enjoy the symphony of pain and delicious screams of primal fear.

A sound erupts, a deep vibrating bellow of a trumpet.

She understands the noise, it was a declaration of war after all.

Anna, the thing that used to be Anna, feels a rare sensation. A trickle of happiness. She will walk in any realm she chooses. She will do whatever she wants to whoever she wants. She will decide to assist the innocent or choose to devour the guilty.

She is judgement. All possibilities exist. Infinite.

She is the ultimate peeler of layers.

She is karma, an eater of sin and vile souls.

She will not bleed her way into new worlds, she is invited.

She belongs.

Truly, there really was purity in her pain.

Revenge indeed.

Anna smiles.

Story notes.

The Void is a world that may be familiar to some, at least, to those who have read my short story The Void in my horror collection Paint it Black.
That particular tale featured a young woman also capable of astral projection. Of course, Bleeding into New worlds is much different.
The concept of out-of-body experiences has fascinated me for a very long time.
Reality, I believe, is far stranger than we can imagine or perhaps ever comprehend.

As for the self-harm aspect, this story is not meant to glamourise in any way.
Thanks for reading
Sarah Jane

READ MORE ABOUT THE VOID IN...

<u>PAINT IT BLACK</u>

Sarah Jane Huntington coats the world in darkness in these thirteen twisted stories. From ghosts to folklore, hauntings to demonic possession, murder to science fiction, take a trip into dark and frightening places.

Also By Sarah Jane Huntington...

<u>BETWEEN LIGHT AND SHADOW</u>

There's a hidden place at the center of all things, a realm of wonder and horror. It exists outside the boundaries of imagination. You'll need an open mind to reach the place *Between Light and Shadow…*

IRON MAIDENS

A 13 story collection of twisted tales, all featuring killer women.Supernatural creations hell bent on revenge. The isolated family with a strange, deep pit on their land and more....Villains, Vigilantes, Voyeurs, and Vengeance.Iron maidens. You won't forget these women.

ABOUT SARAH JANE HUNTINGTON

Writer of horror and other strange supernatural-themed tales.

Mum to a gorgeous rescue dog and several naughty cats.

TWITTER: @sarahjanehunti1

Twitter- @3bpublishing
Instagram- @3bpublishing
www.3-bpublishing.com

Printed in Great Britain
by Amazon

16303022R00106